Meeting Each Other: The Full Story

Raven ShadowHawk

Published in April 2015 by Little Vamp Press

little
vämppress
ISBN: 978-0-9926995-9-8
Cover design by: RavenInk

All characters and words the work of Raven ShadowHawk

All characters, locations, names or incidents appearing in this work are fictitious and a product of the author's overactive imagination. Resemblance to any real persons, living, dead, vampire, ghost, zombie, lycanthrope, faerie or daemon is purely coincidental. Promise.

This book is sexually graphic and intended for a mature audience. This book, and others in the series, should only be purchased and/or read by those for whom it is legal, according to the laws in their country of residence.

DEDICATION

I dedicate this one to my wonderful friends at the Phoenix Writers.

Though you may not know it, your support, critique and humour is a good portion of what made this possible. Wouldn't have dared do it without you.

Cheers guys!

CONTENTS

FOREWORD

Love it or loathe it – though I'm guessing, since you're reading this, that you're in the former camp – erotic fiction is here to stay. It's been around, in one form or another, probably forever. It's not new, but it is changing, evolving, constantly. Markets change, audiences change and ways to read change.

This has never been more true than in recent years. Since writing my dissertation on erotic fiction back in 2005/6, the shift has been drastic. As a society, we're becoming more open-minded, more receptive to this kind of writing. The invention and availability of eReaders has made erotic fiction a great deal more accessible – writers no longer have to rely on big publishers with the money for large print runs and salespeople to get the books into bricks-and-mortar retailers. At the click of a button, you can hold in your hands a huge variety of stories of varying lengths, pairings, subgenres and heat levels. And it's wonderful. It's opened up a whole new world of possibility for readers and writers alike.

As an author, I tend to write whatever I feel like writing – after all, if I'm not enthused about my characters and their stories, how can I expect anyone else to be? But as a reader, editor, and marketer, I do keep an eye on trends. And I've noticed that, in the ten or so years I've been reading erotica and erotic romance, things have been moving towards the kinky. BDSM, spanking, threesomes, sex with strangers and a multitude of other things.

Of course, one person's kink is another person's 'meh,' which is why the variety of erotic fiction available is fantastic – look hard enough and you'll find there really is something to scratch everyone's particular itch. I've covered a fair few kinks, fantasies and fetishes in my own work, and I'm adding more all the time.

I can't really talk about erotic fiction without mentioning *that book*. Again, if you're reading this, I'm pretty sure you know *which book* I'm talking about. That book and its two sequels have also had a huge amount of influence on erotica and erotic romance. Most noticeably the huge upswing in people interested in BDSM-related fiction, which is great for writers with books in that particular subgenre. Not only that, audiences interested in erotica and erotic romance in general have increased.

And that, without writing a bazillion page novel on the topic, can only be a good thing, regardless of one's personal opinion on the trilogy-that-will-not-be-named. In brief . . . hurrah for smut! Long live smut!
Happy reading,
Lucy Felthouse

VICKI & LARA

Though I tried not to notice, I knew, as soon as I entered the bedroom, that Lara was naked. Her clothes lay heaped on the floor beside the bed, damp and stinking of lager.

My breathing hitched and I clicked off the light to hide the blush burning my cheeks.

A few seconds passed before my eyes adjusted, and then I could see everything. Moonlight haloed Lara's body and the bed sheets smoothed the shape of her hips and thighs into soft mounds. Through the cotton, I could see the dark triangle of hair between her legs.

Yep. Totally naked.

I looked away, staring instead at the relative safety of her face.

She stretched, causing the sheets to slip back over her skin. 'Vic?'

'Yes, it's me.' I licked my lips, my gaze following the scalloped edge of the sheet as it inched further down her body. When it dropped off the peak of her breasts and landed in a rumpled pile on her stomach, my own gut clenched.

The cool air teased Lara's dark nipples into stiffness and brought goose pimples to my arms. Her hair, red and long, slithered over her neck and shoulders, shiny in the silver light falling through the open curtains.

'Are you sure you don't want a T-shirt?' I pulled open a drawer on my dresser, eager to cover her up. To remove the temptation.

'You really think you have anything to fit me, Miss Hips-and-Arse? Don't worry about it.' Grinning, she shook her head and lifted a corner of the sheet in that universal gesture of invitation. 'Coming?'

'Just a second.'

Rough red lace with a plunging neckline made the first nightdress I found unacceptable. Better was the white tent-like garment with a pair of sleeping teddy bears stitched onto the chest.

1

Perfect.

I took time over removing my jewellery; placing each item on the dresser in a neat line. Over the back of the chair, I draped my skirt, then my blouse, aware that Lara followed my every move. Only after turning my back and wriggling into the nightshirt did I take the time to fold the clothes.

'You okay, hon?'

Still facing the door, I took a deep breath. 'Fine.'

'Is everyone gone now?'

I nodded. 'Bill's got the spare room. Lin, Niall and Carol are sharing the sitting room.'

'In you get, then.'

When I turned back, Lara lifted the sheet. She held it high and gestured with her free hand, renewing the invitation. 'You're leaving your underwear on?'

'Yes.' I said, pleased at how steady my voice sounded.

'You'll ruin the bra.'

'It's fine.'

She shrugged. 'Whatever.'

No more excuses.

I stepped up to the bed, arms folded across my chest. Swallowing the lump of my heart in my throat, I climbed in and tucked my half of the sheets around me. Six inches of mattress separated me from Lara's naked body.

Not enough.

She rolled her eyes, then turned onto her side to face me. Her eyes shone like liquid crystal while moonlight highlighted the bright white of her teeth and gave her the impression of a Cheshire cat.

'Thanks for hiding my car keys,' she said.

'No problem.'

Lara propped her head on one hand and traced small circles on the sheet with the other. Each time her finger came close to my side, my chest tightened. I moved my hands away and clasped them on top of my stomach instead.

The finger stopped moving. 'Had a good time?'

'I guess. No puke, fights or arrests. That must be a record.'

'For one of your birthdays? Probably.'

The next words seemed to burn my mouth as they left it. 'What happened to Malcolm?'

'What do you mean?'

I stared at her. 'He looked . . . upset.'

'I suppose he would have been. But not as much as you.'

She was right about that, so I kept my mouth shut.

Lara grinned and flopped onto her back.

With my peripheral vision, I saw the sheet slide off her breasts again. It took vast strength of will to keep my eyes on her face. Despite that, my mouth moistened and my body tightened as I imagined touching her nipples with my tongue. I could almost feel the silk-like softness of her skin against my lips and palms. Her smooth, pale body above my dark one.

'—creep with a jealousy complex. He deserved it.'

Only from the silence that followed did I realise Lara was expecting a reply.

'Were you even listening?'

'Sorry. Miles away.'

'I'll say. I said he deserved it. He's not your boyfriend any more, just a creep with a jealousy complex. Why do you think I did it?'

'You're crazy, that's why.'

'No.' She grinned. 'I did it because he thinks you're stupid. That you'd go back to him after how he treated you.'

'He said that?'

'Near enough. But I knew you wouldn't.'

Lara's gaze was hot on mine, eyes widening. I recognised the signs; I knew she was trying to tell me something. Part of me wanted her to simply say it, but the rest of me worried what the words would be. So I didn't ask. Instead, I settled on something safer.

'But did you have to shave his head?'

She grinned, and the gesture sent slithers of warmth coursing through my body, as far as my toes.

'It'll grow back.'

In my mind's eye, I saw Malcolm storm from the house, fingering the inch-wide strip of exposed skin along his skull from forehead to the nape of his neck.

'Feeling sorry for him?'

'God no, I just—' I had no words to finish the thought.

'Vic, you're my girl. You must know I'm going to stand up for you. Whatever happens.'

My girl.

The words gave me a warm glow I had no right to feel.

A smile played around my lips. My shoulders relaxed into the mattress. 'What did you do with it?'

'The ponytail? Binned it; mullets went out years ago. Why? Did you want a souvenir?'

'Gross!'

Chuckling, Lara pantomimed her earlier actions with the razor. 'Bzz!' she cried, jabbing the air near my face with a bunched-up fist. 'Let's see him fix *that* without going for a complete skin-head!'

'Thank you.'

3

'Don't be stupid.' Lara reached over and yanked me into a bone-crunching hug. She seemed not to notice when I stiffened beneath her. A twist of her hips pressed her whole body against mine.

Her nearness made my nightshirt pointless. I felt everything, from the heat of her skin, to the patch of sweat on her chest and stomach. Her breath whispered across my face: cheap wine laced with chicken Madras, mango chutney and cheap lipstick.

I closed my eyes and inhaled.

'I love you, Vic.'

My eyes snapped open.

I jerked away, spitting strands of her red hair from my mouth. 'What?' I wiped sweaty palms on the front of my nightshirt and tried to tell the joyous leap in my stomach that she couldn't possibly mean what I hoped she did.

'You're my best friend,' she continued. 'I don't know what I'd do without you.'

'You're drunk. Anyway, it's more like what *I'd* do without *you*.' I frowned. 'Malcolm would have—'

Tension rushed back into my body. The gut-churning sensation of impotent fear crawled through my limbs as they remembered the feel of his large calloused hands gripping my arm. Pulling me around.

I pressed my legs together.

'How did you know where we were?'

'You looked so scared, I followed you,' she said. 'No one else noticed.'

'Good.'

'It's not. People need to know what he's like. He's lucky Bill didn't see.'

I tried to imagine the night's outcome if my brother had found out what Malcolm had done. 'It would continue the trend of birthday arrests.'

Lara smirked. 'But Malcolm isn't worth going to prison over. So I dealt with it.' She patted my shoulder and peace oozed through me.

The tiny hairs on my arms and legs stood to attention beneath my nightshirt. Blood rushed to the surface and flushed my skin with heat.

'Hey, Vic, it's okay. He's gone now.' She spoke to me the same way she spoke to children on the ward. I imagined her standing over me in her pale-yellow uniform, bright hair pulled off her face in a high ponytail. It's true what they say about nurses.

'I'm fine.'

'Then why are you shaking? Come here.' She curled her limbs around me again, tucking her head beneath my chin and rubbing my arms with brisk strokes.

'I'm not cold.'

Lara ignored me. 'You always react badly to booze. Remember Majorca?'

I did, and the memory was the last one I needed at that moment: Lara's scantily clad body, writhing to music, dripping with sweat. The rising warmth in my belly. The first understanding that my feelings for my best friend were evolving into something more. Something unexpected. Something needy and visceral.

I remembered our drunken kiss on the heaving dance floor and the playful press of her hands on my hips and ribs as we teased the Spanish men and their shameless stares.

My body hummed with a pulsing need and a trickle of wetness slid down the inside of my thighs. I wrenched free gulping air. My back left the mattress and I clawed at the empty air, too late to save myself from falling off the side of the bed. The sheet followed. Pooling on my face as my hip and shoulder slammed into the floor. My feet dangled in the air, ankles skimming the mattress.

Lara's voice shook with laughter. 'You okay?'

I closed my eyes beneath the sheet, glad of something to hide behind. 'Fine.'

'I bet you drank more than I did.'

The sheet tickled as it left my face. Lara had crawled up to the edge of the bed and she held it bunched up in front of her, pressed between her spread knees as she knelt to stare at me. Her expression held a mixture of amusement and concern. And one last thing that I couldn't place. Whatever it was, it made me uncomfortable.

I looked away from her face, but that was worse.

I saw the gleaming nimbus of moonshine around her body. Light playing over the curves of her hips and thighs in a way that made my fingers jealous. An angel, beautiful and desirable, naked breasts a mere inch from my upturned face.

Clambering to my feet felt harder than it should have been, and I fussed with the hem of my nightshirt.

'Are you really going to leave your bra on?'

I frowned. The back of my neck tingled, and I told myself that it was wishful thinking, nothing more, that put an undercurrent of disappointment in Lara's whisper.

She sighed and made space by shuffling back across the bed. While she stretched out on the far side, shaking the sheet over her body once again, I took my old place on the edge; with that six-inch chasm between us.

This time, she didn't turn to look at me.

I pulled the sheet over my body and tried to think of something to say.

Silence stretched between us like a piece of elastic, growing thinner all the while.

Lara faced the ceiling and closed her eyes. Soon, her breathing evened out and the gentle rise and fall of her chest told me she had fallen asleep.

Turning on to my side, I propped my head in my hand. I let my gaze travel up and down her body, drinking in the sight with a greed that frightened and excited me.

Sleep brought to Lara a peace and beauty for which her waking features had no space. Not that she was any less beautiful while awake, only that her bright smile and open-mouthed laughter often left no room to appreciate the delicate curve of her cheekbones. The full pout of her lips. The thick sweep of her eyelashes. The arch of her eyebrows showing off her natural colour which hid beneath all the red.

A curl of her hair lay like a crimson shadow across her cheek. I brushed it away.

In the still of the bedroom, I heard my heart hammering my ribs. It seemed impossible for the thunderous crashes not to disturb Lara's sleep. The torrent of blood pumping through my veins filled my ears until it masked even the sound of my breathing.

I sat up and pulled the sheet. Gently, then faster, exposing Lara's body with the same reverence as a sculptor showing off his final, finest work. Lara's bare body resembled a piece of fine art. Smooth and perfect, dappled with an ethereal glow sliced by shadows.

My hand hovered above her stomach, a finger's breadth from touching. The tiniest motion from either of us would bring my skin into contact with hers.

The thought made me grind my legs together.

'Lara?'

No answer.

A combination of drink and darkness made me bold.

I touched her stomach. Felt the gentle rise beneath my fingers as she inhaled. Her skin, as I'd imagined, was petal-soft beneath my trembling digits.

The lack of colour in her skin against mine startled me. So very pale. Or was I overly dark? I couldn't tell, but I knew that touch alone couldn't and wouldn't satisfy my growing need. I trailed my fingers towards her ribs; allowed my palm to brush the underside of her breasts.

She sighed.

Looking at her face again, I saw the little line of moisture between her lips stretch and break as they parted. A tiny piece of her tongue, pale-pink and wet, showed through the gap.

Common sense, what little I had, fled. It left a hole in my mind, quickly filled by a rush of lust that raged and roiled inside.

I kissed her lips.

A gust of warm air flew from her nostrils and tickled my face.

'Fuck me,' I whispered.

'If you like.'

I reeled back, yelping like a puppy with its tail stuck in the door.

Lara didn't move, but stared at me through half-lidded eyes. Her mouth twitched.

'You were asleep!'

'Was I?'

I scrambled off the bed, still clumsy, but more graceful than my last descent. The sheets tangled in my legs, pinning me in place. Forced to kick them away, I lost precious seconds of my escape. By the time I'd freed myself, Lara had sat up and turned to stare at me. She didn't bother to cover herself.

'I'm so sorry.' The words tumbled out. 'I didn't mean to. I mean, I shouldn't have. I had no right. You were sleeping, I just—'

'Just what, Vic? Thought you'd feel me up?' She arched an eyebrow at me, that curious expression back in her eyes again.

At last I managed to identify the look. A challenge.

'It wasn't like that!'

'Then what *was* it like?'

'I don't know. God, I'm sorry. I'll go.'

'Where?' An edge of weariness crept into her tone. 'This is your room. Anyway, the house is crammed – that's why I'm here.'

'You're here because you're drunk.'

'Other nights I've slept on the sofa, but today you said sleep in here. Why would you do that, Vic? Tell me.'

I opened my mouth, but no words came out. Instead, my fingers twisted once more into the hem of my nightshirt. I heard the cotton tear and yanked my hands away. With nowhere left to put them, I crossed my arms and hid them in my armpits.

She stared at me. 'Vicki, say something.'

I caught her eye, then looked at the floor. 'Like what?'

'You invite me in here, but won't touch me. You watch me strip, but run off before I can finish. You come back and put on a nightshirt. A fucking nightshirt! Then you refuse to even take your bra off.'

'I'm sorry.'

'Don't be sorry, Vic, tell me what you want. Or for once, do something.'

'Like what?'

'Anything!' She slapped the bed sheets with her palm.

This time, when my mouth opened, I managed a small squeak. Something clamped down on my words and stopped them from escaping and, as I looked at Lara, I knew I couldn't do it. I turned and walked to the door.

A loud thud told me Lara had jumped off the bed. She reached the door before I did and slammed her hand flat against it. I tugged the handle, but couldn't open it more than an inch.

'Stop running away!'

I tried the door again, and this time Lara stepped right into my back. She pressed into me, her body forming a hot contour of joined skin against my spine. Her fingers closed over mine and yanked them away from the handle.

'Let go, Lara.'

'Talk to me.'

'I can't.'

'You can. It's me. You can say anything to me.'

When I jerked my hand out of hers and returned it to the handle, Lara growled. She jerked forward and shoved me against the door. Though her head only reached my shoulder, her strength in that moment was utterly foreign and made my heart jump in my chest. No way to tell how much of that was fear and how much was excitement.

She pushed both hands under the bottom of my nightshirt and caressed my hips in one long bold stroke.

My knees quivered, then hit the door. Her fingers left a line of fire on my body that stopped where her hands did, just beneath the wire of my stupid, stupid bra.

I pushed back. Faced her. Lowered my head and crushed my lips against hers in a deep kiss made of longing and frustration.

I had no idea who was more surprised.

When I pulled back, her eyes were wide and bright. Her hands hovered in the air, a short way from my face as though she meant to touch me.

The bears on my nightshirt leapt up and down and only then did I realise that the strained panting I could hear came from me. I licked my lips and pulled a slow breath through my nostrils.

'Sorry.'

'If you apologise one more time, I'm leaving.'

'Sor— Okay.' I closed my eyes for a second, squeezing the lids together so tightly that white and purple rings danced through the blackness. When I opened them again, Lara was still there, staring up at me with an expression of mingled exasperation and amusement.

'Feel better?'

'A little.'

She kissed me, far softer than I had done her, but longer, and somehow more verbose than anything else she'd said that night. 'Was that so bad?' Her hand cupped my face while her thumb stroked my cheek. 'Please talk to me.'

My eyes scrunched closed, as if to shut her out would make speaking easier. 'I'm scared.'

The room became still. Only the light brush of her skin against my face let me know she was still there.

'Why?'

8

'I'm not your type.'

'What are you talking about?'

I opened my eyes a crack. Through the gap, Lara stared at me; beautiful lips slightly parted, eyes wide. 'I'm nothing like other girls you've dated. And I didn't think you'd be interested because of Malcolm.'

Lara's hand slid over my jaw. Though I tried to resist, she forcibly turned my face to hers. Gentle kisses touched my forehead, nose and chin. Then my lips.

'I'm naked, Vic. I've been trying to get your clothes off since you came in. You're the one resisting. Not me.'

I hadn't realised I was crying until she brushed the tears away.

'Come here.'

I leaned against her, the heat of her body a long line of comfort and security against my face and chest. My arms curled around her, meeting between her shoulder blades. Eager hands stroked my ribs then clutched me close, fingers kneading me through my nightshirt.

When she kissed me, it felt better than I ever could have imagined. I compared those first kisses to something good, but weak, like a single piano chord or a recorder. This kiss was a full opus with an entire orchestra, filled with melody and rhythm and stories of a desire so strong I felt them brush my skin like warm fur.

Her tongue traced a delicate pattern around the inside of my mouth; probing, teasing, exploratory, but gentle. She tasted so good, even through the stale flavour of wine and curry that lingered on her lips. Most of all, Lara tasted of herself, and that was a flavour I'd remember and savour for years to come.

One of her small long-fingered hands slipped beneath the hem of my nightshirt. The tips of her fingers touched my thigh and pulled a shudder out of me that rippled all the way down my spine. 'What are you doing?'

'Vicki, please.' Her voice trembled with a fevered need I'd never heard before. 'I want to touch you.'

A fluttering sensation, like the sensual beat of butterfly wings, tickled through my stomach. My nipples tightened. My head swam. All this and she'd barely touched me at all.

'Where?' I asked.

She gave me a look. Then she pulled the nightshirt up my thighs and bunched it above my hips, exposing my knickers. 'Here.' Her free hand stroked my stomach, just above the line of the elastic. 'Here.' The line of my ribs beneath the bra. 'And will you take this fucking thing off?'

Her impatience was so normal that for a moment I forgot what we were doing. I threw back my head and laughed.

The nightshirt took seconds to remove. The bra, less.

Standing before Lara, naked but for my knickers, I realised, for the first time, how much she wanted me. Her eyes were huge and shiny in the darkness. Filled with hunger. A sigh rushed from her lips and she held her hand about an inch from my body, as if afraid to close that meagre distance and finally touch.

'What's wrong?'

'I just want to savour this for a second.'

'I'm going to lose my nerve if you don't hurry up.'

She giggled.

'I mean it. Come here.' I snatched her hand, cupped it against my breast, then mirrored the gesture on the other side.

Standing before Lara, holding her palms against my nipples, my own body tingled and shivered. A cotton-soft ball of pleasure gathered in my stomach, stirring round and spinning out thin tendrils of pleasure to seep through my limbs in wriggling threads of warmth.

My pulse filled the back of my throat.

Her thumbs traced a slow path around my nipples, round and round until they stood out towards her. A sigh fell out of her mouth, followed by a low groan. She gripped me, a tiny squeeze, then relaxed; a motion that went through her body from the shoulders down.

Grinning, Lara sank to her knees. She trailed her hand over my body the whole way down and, though my breasts felt suddenly cold and exposed, I couldn't find the will to complain. Her lips traced a path down my stomach, licking and kissing every inch of the way; even the stretch marks around my belly button.

She batted at my hands when I tried to cover up.

'Stop it.'

'Then leave the stretch marks alone.'

'But I like the way they feel.'

'They're ugly.'

'No part of you is ugly. Trust me.'

The argument died on my lips when Lara hooked her fingers into the sides of my damp knickers and eased them down. She watched my face the whole time, the tip of her tongue peeping out the corner of her mouth as she slipped the elastic over the generous curve of my hips and thighs.

She lifted my feet, one by one, to help me out of them, then dropped them somewhere behind her.

Those thin threads of pleasure spread faster through my body.

She gazed at my fully-naked body and licked her lips.

'You're smooth.' The passion in her voice caressed parts of me that no physical hand could ever touch. Then she did touch me; the lightest of fingertip strokes through the hairless moisture. 'I can't believe how wet you are.'

This time I did cover myself.

'I'm taking it as a compliment, Vic, don't worry. This is wonderful.'

'It's embarrassing.'

'It shouldn't be. Here.' She stood with one swift bounce and took my hand. Gaze hot on mine, she pressed my fingers between her legs and rubbed. 'Fuck,' she hissed.

If any capacity to speak had remained with me I might have echoed her. As it was, the feel of her own desire, slick against my fingers, stole my voice and snatched a groan from the back of my throat. When I did speak it was a whisper. 'You really do want me.'

'Jesus, Vic, I can't say it any clearer than that. Come over here.' She crossed to the bed and knelt on it.

I rushed to join her, perching on the end with my feet on the floor.

Lara eased me back against the pillows and picked up my feet, swivelling me round until I lay flat. After another sweet kiss, she slithered down my body and put her hands on my thighs.

She looked at me and, though her eyes were hot with passion, I knew she was waiting for me.

I nodded. My breathing caught and I had to swallow several times before I could speak. 'Go ahead.'

Smiling, she tucked both hands between my thighs and eased them apart. Lara watched my face the whole time, the crease of a frown showing between her eyebrows. 'You okay?'

'I feel—' But I couldn't find the words I wanted. None were big enough. I settled for, 'I'm nervous.'

'Don't be.' She rubbed my stomach, tender and lingering. Her touch soothed me.

Then Lara leaned over and pressed her mouth against mine. Her lips were soft, slightly rough on the bottom where her lower lip had cracked. I caught the smell of wine and lipstick again and beneath it, the heady scent of Lara's own body. Then her warm tongue snaked past the barrier of my teeth and once more into my mouth. Her touch caressed me in the same way her voice had and made my body twist and writhe.

Pleasure made me giddy. I moaned as a tingle grew in my toes and crept up through my body an inch at a time.

My hands flapped awkwardly until Lara took them and placed them on her back. I rested my fingers on her shoulder blades.

'Relax.'

Perhaps she saw the struggle in my face because she rolled her eyes and sat up, straddling my hips. She arched her back and straightened her shoulders to show off her beautiful breasts.

My mind swam with the desire to touch, kiss, bite, suck. Anything I could do to bring my skin into contact with hers.

'Touch me,' she begged.

I craned forward far enough to kiss one tempting nipple. That single taste eclipsed the rest of my worries and I sucked more of her breast into my mouth.

Lara gasped. She pressed her hips against me. 'Good,' she hissed. 'Again.'

I obeyed, the other nipple this time, following up with a gentle bite. I rolled that hard nipple between my teeth. Lara's thighs trembled. My head flopped back. She clambered over my body and braced her hands on either side of my head, expression taut with lust. The need in her face rubbed my senses raw until the slightest sound or touch was enough to set me alight. Again her hands cupped my breasts, repeating that flicking, thumbing motion which made me squirm.

My hands dropped to the bed and tangled in the sheets.

Lara's lips touched my chin, my neck, my shoulders, finally travelling down until the heat of her breath billowed over my left nipple. The little nub of flesh rose immediately to meet her and she sucked it into her mouth. With a gentle, kneading motion, her right hand continued to massage the other breast. Her left hand drifted down.

It whispered over my ribs, my stomach. Paused briefly to tickle the indent of my belly button. Moved on to the base of my abdomen. Then the hand stopped, fingertips resting on my skin.

'Close your eyes.'

I shut my eyes after a few moments' hesitation and bit my lip when I felt both of her hands leave my body. When they returned, it was to grip my feet and push; bending my legs at the knee until my feet lay flat on the bed well over a metre apart.

Being so thoroughly exposed brought a flood of heat to my face. I opened my eyes and looked down to see Lara kneeling between my legs, head down, lips parted, eyes hungry.

'Lara?'

She kissed my knees and shins. 'Do you trust me?'

'I suppose so.'

'I guess I'll just have to take that, if it's the best you can give me.'

I giggled. My stiff legs relaxed. 'I *do* trust you.'

'I'll stop any time you want. But if you let me start . . . you won't want me to.'

'I don't want you to stop.'

'Then stop interrupting!' She chuckled and caught her balance on my knees. Her hair tickled my thighs as she leaned further forward.

This time I could feel the heat of her breath, rhythmically puffing against the wet, central spot already sensitised almost beyond endurance. Cool air met my sweaty flesh, and I fought the urge to grind my legs together. The jumble of opposites made me wetter than ever, and I felt the evidence of my passion slide down my shaved skin and drip onto the sheets.

'Lara?'

The first flicker of her tongue made me buck my hips and forget whatever I'd intended to say. My yelp trailed off into a soft, keening moan when she started a languid stroking motion, so slow it was ecstatic torture.

My fingers clamped down on my hair. More sweat beaded on my forehead, trickling down my face to gather in the corner of my mouth like a tear. When I parted my lips to groan again, it slipped into my mouth and vanished on my tongue in a tiny burst of salt.

My toes became numb.

Between my legs, Lara made soft, happy noises and gently massaged my thighs. When I finally managed to open my eyes, I could just see the top of her head, bobbing up and down in time with her lapping tongue.

The warmth, the tingling, the incredible pressure swelled and oozed through me like ink on blotting paper. Fingers of electric pleasure brought tears to my eyes.

When Lara's first finger slipped inside me, my hips rocked up and forwards, slamming against her face, grinding my pubis against her mouth.

She nibbled me with her front teeth.

'Lara!'

Another finger joined the first and my back arched off the bed.

Ecstasy built like a rockslide, gathering more and more power as it passed. The sensations built into an avalanche, threatening to flatten all rational thought as it ploughed over me and buried me in bliss.

Lara's tongue lapped at the very heart of me and worked a magic that guided me to the edge and hurled me into space where stars danced gold and bright behind my closed eyelids.

I shouted – one wordless exclamation as something buried deep inside boiled up and spilled over in a welcomed and much-needed release. It saturated my bones, broke a fresh sweat on my skin and made my legs shudder like runaway prisoners caught on an electric fence.

Lara moved with my writhing motions, gripping my thighs and pressing down to hold me steady. She continued to lick me, suck me and nibble me, not noticing, or maybe not caring that I could scarcely breathe.

Another yelp escaped me; shrill and frantic.

I jerked free and snapped my legs together. 'Stop, stop, please!'

'Did I hurt you?' She stared at me over the bumps of my knees. Her mouth glistened. Her eyes narrowed with worry.

I laughed. My hips dropped down to rest against the mattress for the first time in half an hour. 'Are you kidding? I can't breathe.' I hid my face.

'Please.' Lara snorted. 'Don't try to make me believe you've not had an orgasm before. What about that massager you got for your last birthday?'

I forced myself upright. 'Never like that. I've had toys and Malcolm was good for something, but that was new.' I made my voice low, catching Lara's gaze and holding it.

She cocked an eyebrow at me.

'Honest. Never like that.'

'Because I'm a girl?'

'Partly. Or maybe it was just that good.'

I laughed at her sceptical look and gathered her into my arms. Lying on the bed, smiling into the half-darkness, I combed my fingers through that long, red hair. 'And it might be new, but you've given me lots of ideas on how to return the favour.'

The ravenous look in Lara's eyes was the best gift of the night so far.

CAROL, NIALL & LIN

Carol gazed at the food-littered floor and sighed. Her shoulders slumped. 'This isn't the setting I had in mind for this.'

'What was that, love?'

'Nothing.' She closed her eyes, counted to ten, then turned to find Niall.

He sprawled on the sofa in that classic guy pose: legs open, feet flat on the floor. One long arm draped around the shoulders of a small, pale woman, Lin, with her elegant hair and trendy designer glasses to match her equally trendy asymmetric dress.

'When do we start?' he asked.

Lin shrugged beneath his arm. 'Whenever you like. This is your arrangement, yes? You choose.'

'Thanks,' Carol snapped. 'That's good of you.'

A glacial stare from her boyfriend told her he'd noticed the bite in her words.

'Excuse us for a second, Lin,' he said.

'Of course.' She looked away, twirling the rings on her thumb and little finger.

'Carol?' Niall stood and pointed to the far corner of the room.

Sighing, Carol followed him there and slouched beside the TV. Careful to put her back to Lin, she crossed her arms. 'What?'

'What's wrong with you? You're all tense.'

'I'm not.'

He frowned. 'This is what you wanted, right?'

The answer froze on her tongue.

'Talk to me.' He reached toward her, stroking the back of his hand down her arm.

Carol grasped his fingers and squeezed. Instead of trying to put her thoughts into words, she raised the fingers to her lips and kissed them.

The living room door opened.

'Hey, guys.' Vicki poked her head into the room. 'Have you seen Jasper?'

After scanning the ground at ankle level, Carol shook her head. 'You sure he's in here?'

'I think so. I can't find him anywhere else. If you see him, put him out, will you?'

'Sure.'

'Thanks.' Vicki lingered in the doorway, drumming the wood with her fingernails.

Carol watched her. 'You okay?'

'Yes I— Yes. I am.' The woman shook herself. 'Just checking on you. Sorry there's no sleeping bags.'

'Oh, we'll be fine.' Niall smiled and walked to the sofa. He perched on the end and kicked off his boots. 'I'm sure the three of us will be cosy enough.'

Lin snickered.

A frown furrowed Vicki's brow. 'Okay. I guess I'll go then.'

Carol hitched a smile on to her face. 'We're fine, honest. Get some rest. You look shattered. Happy birthday, by the way.'

'Thanks. Goodnight.' Vicki turned and shut the door behind her.

Niall immediately turned to Lin and touched her hand. She smiled and opened her fingers, letting him trace a path over her palm.

Carol gritted her teeth. 'We'd better get ready for bed.'

'What?' Niall stopped stroking.

'I want some sleep.'

He gaped at her. 'But I thought we were going to . . . what about our . . . you know?'

'We're not doing any of that tonight.'

'Why?'

'I don't think we should.'

'But why?' He pouted. 'Wasn't that the point of all this?'

Carol kicked at a pizza box on her way to the sofa. Standing behind it she peered down at Lin. The smaller woman gazed back, dark eyes thoughtful behind her glasses.

A wriggle of discomfort wormed through Carol's stomach. She looked at Niall instead. From the corner of her eye she could still see Lin. Staring. 'We need to get to know each other first.'

Lin combed delicate fingers through her hair. 'I thought we had. We've been talking for weeks, yes?'

'Online.'

Niall sat a little straighter. 'Online, yes, but tonight too. We've been talking all night, love.'

'And we talked on the phone,' Lin added.

'Webcam conversations.'

With each fresh point, Carol tilted her chin higher. By the time they finished, she had both arms wrapped around her body and her gaze pinned to the opposite wall. 'Fine,' she snapped, 'I know all that. But we're in Vicki's house. We shouldn't. Not after she just broke up with Malcolm.'

'Weeks ago!' said Niall.

She shrugged.

Lin stood. The smaller woman didn't speak, simply crossed the room to retrieve a half-pint plastic cup from the cabinet beside the TV. She sipped it and watched them both over the rim.

'Look,' he continued, 'Vicki seems fine to me. Getting back on the horse pretty damn quick, if you know what I mean.'

Carol gave him a blank look.

'Didn't you see her drooling at Lara?'

'What?'

'God, you're blind when you want to be. Forget it.'

Carol stared at her hands. She took a deep breath. 'Niall—'

A leaping streak of black-and-white fur cut her off. She had just enough time to register it was Jasper before he bounded off the cushions and pounced on Lin, clawing her knees and shins.

With a cry, Lin dropped the cup. The contents splashed her dress and shoes as well as the cat, which hissed and lashed out with his claws extended.

'I've got him.' Niall dived off the sofa and grabbed the soggy feline by the tail. 'Bloody thing. Out with you.' Straining to avoid teeth and claws, he scooped up the struggling cat and marched to the door. 'Be right back.' He fled, taking the yowling creature with him.

Despite the initial spike of vindictive pleasure, when Carol next looked at Lin, she winced. Lager dripped from her sassy red dress, and several ladders ran down her tights. 'You okay?'

Lin glanced up. 'Are you?'

'Excuse me?'

The pause between them held a charge, like clouds before a lightning storm.

Carol fought the dense quality of the air with a few deep breaths. Without Niall to form a bridge between them the room felt large and impassable. 'Well?'

Lin looked away first. 'It's nothing.' She shook her head. 'I'm fine. Just scratched.' The tights sagged around her legs. 'My clothes – they're ruined.'

'Sorry about that.'

'It's not your fault. Maybe I can rinse the dress.'

'I'm sure Vicki won't mind.'

'Good.' Kicking off her shoes, Lin turned on the spot and pointed to the middle of her back. 'Can you get the zip for me?'

Carol rubbed her hands against her jeans. 'You can't reach it yourself?'

'No. Please?'

'Fine.' A step forward. Close enough to see the subtle highlights of blue in Lin's hair. A light dusting of freckles speckled the backs of her shoulders.

Carol caught the subtle whiff of jasmine and vanilla and took a moment to enjoy the delicate smells. Lin's own scent lingered underneath with a hint of the lager she'd been drinking all night.

Shaking aside the curious diversion, Carol grabbed the zip and yanked it down. 'There.' She jerked her hands back.

'Thank you.' Lin stepped away, pulling the straps off her shoulders as she went. She reached the living room door and walked through, easing the dress down her ribs.

'Fuck. What's wrong with me?' Hands shaking, Carol turned away and stared at the blank eye of the TV. 'This is stupid. So fucking stupid.' She pressed her hands against her face to stop them shaking. 'This was my idea. Get a grip.' Cupping her sweaty palms to her cheeks eventually stilled them.

By the time Niall returned she felt a little more like herself.

'I hate cats,' he hissed, dabbing a tissue against a scratch on his jaw. 'Where's Lin?'

'Soaking her dress.'

The silence between them made Carol's skin itch. Not the same type of discomfort she'd felt with Lin, but close.

She tried to smile and failed. Bending down, she scooped up empty crisp packets and plastic cups to shove into the soggy pizza boxes.

Most of the room was clear before Niall blocked her path. 'What are you doing, love?'

'Cleaning up.'

'Talk to me.'

She bit her lip. 'I'm fine.'

'Oh, really?'

'Yes.'

He sighed. 'What do you think of Lin?'

'She's lovely.'

'But . . .?'

'But nothing.'

He arched an eyebrow. 'I think she's nice. Hot, right?'

The last pizza box crumpled beneath Carol's tightening grip. 'If you like skinny Chinese women.'

'I do actually.'

She hurled the box to the floor. 'Great. Good for you.'

'Carol, what the hell?'

Twisting away from his hands, she stomped over to the sofa and threw herself on to it. She crossed her legs. Folded her arms tight across her chest. Glared at Niall. 'You've been all over her all night. What am I supposed to think? To feel?'

'Carol—'

'No!' Like juicing a lemon, Carol let all her sour thoughts flood free. 'I know what we planned, but it's different when it's in your face. I don't know if I can watch you touch her like you touch me. You're mine, Niall.'

'Now wait just a minute, love.' He dropped to his knees beside the sofa. 'I'm never going to touch Lin like I touch you. I've never going to touch another woman like that.'

She laughed, but it was a bitter sound. 'Isn't that the point of a threesome?'

'No, love.' He shook his head. 'I mean I'm never going to touch Lin like I touch you because I don't feel the same way about her. She's just spice.'

'What's that supposed to mean?'

'Spice on a meal that already tastes good and would be just as good, if not better, without it.'

'What the hell are you talking about?'

'You, love. You're the meal. And I don't need *her* to make *you* better. I love you.'

The tide of Carol's anger hit a wall. She looked at him. 'Yeah?'

'Of course I bloody do! Carol,' he put a hand on her knee, 'I agreed to this because I thought *you* wanted it. We don't *have* to do anything tonight.'

'But Lin . . . You've been touching her all night. Flirting. Eric tried to talk to you about football, and you wouldn't even look at him.'

'Sex versus footie. It's a close call, but the sex wins.' He said it as though it explained everything.

'I want to do it. I just didn't realise how hard it would be.'

'Then take it slow, love. Try to relax a bit. Nothing's going to happen unless we're all happy.' The hand on her knee slipped down her calf, massaging the tight knot of muscle there. 'Okay?'

Carol closed her eyes. 'Okay.'

When she opened her eyes again, Niall had raised himself on to his knees. He pushed both hands along the outsides of her thighs and leaned forward. 'Kiss.'

She bent to meet him, pressing her lips to his. His stubble scratched her chin and jaw, and she heard him sigh in response.

'I'm sorry.' She whispered the words against his cheek.

'Don't be.'

He pushed her sideways and lifted her legs on to the sofa so that she lay across it. Carol reached up and pulled him down to meet her, then grinned when he joined her on the narrow cushions. His weight pinned her in place.

Another kiss.

'You taste like pizza,' she said.

'And you taste like cider.'

Niall's hands found the bottom of her top and lifted it, giving his hands free passage to her skin. She shivered as he traced a pattern around the indent of her belly button.

'Wait.'

'What?' He stopped.

'I don't want Lin to see us like this.'

'Embarrassed?'

'No, but she might be.'

'I doubt a woman like her would get embarrassed over a little kissing.'

Carol shook her head. 'You don't know that.'

'I know enough.' Niall pushed back on to one side of the sofa. 'You really think the type of woman who'd be embarrassed over kissing would sign up to a site like Fetlife to find a threesome? Hell, would she meet up with two strangers for the sole purpose of screwing them both? Don't think so, love.'

The living room door opened while Carol thought about it. She looked up in time to see Lin hurry through and press it shut behind her.

The dress and tights were gone. In their place, Lin wore a blue dressing gown, long enough to brush the tops of her bare feet. With the sleeves rolled up, thick bunches of fabric still managed to swallow her hands as far as her fingertips.

'It's very noisy upstairs,' she murmured, gazing at the floor.

Carol pulled herself into a sitting position. 'Is it Vicki? Is she okay?'

'Not Vicki, the other room.'

'Isn't that where Bill is?' Niall glanced at the ceiling.

'Bill?' Lin frowned.

'Vicki's brother.'

'Oh.' She grinned, showing off straight, white teeth. 'That explains it.'

'What? Is he okay?'

'He's fine. He's . . . busy.'

'Busy how?' Carol's voice was sharper than she wanted it to be, but something about Lin's knowing smile made her want to ball her hands into fists.

The other woman gave her a steady look. 'Busy wanking. In front of a film, probably. I heard *porn noises*,' she made quote marks with her fingers. 'And moaning.'

Carol's mouth dropped open.

Niall snorted. 'Seriously?'

'Oh, yes.'

'I thought he was chasing Simone,' said Carol.

20

Another laugh from Niall, again disguised as a snort. 'You think that means he doesn't do porn? You know men better than that.'

Carol rallied, shaking her head. She inhaled and released the breath slowly through her mouth. Directing her attention at Lin's new attire, rather than the illicit happenings upstairs, seemed far safer. 'Where did you get that?'

If surprised by the change in subject, Lin didn't show it. She pulled the dressing gown tighter around her. 'Bathroom. On the back of the door. Vicki won't mind, yes? I'll check the dress later.'

Silence consumed the room.

Through it came the sound of low voices from directly overhead. The mumble of conversation in the room upstairs faded, replaced seconds later by a loud moan of pleasure.

'Bill?' Carol looked at Niall, but it was Lin who answered.

'No, a woman. Two women.'

Niall grinned. 'Vicki and Lara. I knew it.'

Another moan came through the ceiling, then a loud cry, followed by sporadic pounding and the frantic creak of bed springs.

'Oh, Jesus.' Carol buried her face in her hands.

'What? You don't want to be disrespectful to your friend, but as host she sets the boundaries, yes?' Lin glanced at the ceiling. She smiled. 'If she can have sex upstairs and her brother can watch porn all night, why can't we do what we came to do?'

'Doesn't it feel icky to you?'

'No.'

'We don't even have a bed.'

Lin shrugged. 'Beds are personal. Even our homes are too personal for what we're planning. Neutral space is good. Less conflict, yes?'

'She has a point, love.'

Carol opened her mouth. Closed it. By the time she looked out from beneath her hands, Lin had moved close enough to touch. She quickly put her hands in her lap, trying, without success, to close her senses to that faint scent of vanilla and jasmine.

'Carol, I've never done this either. But Fetlife is for trying new things. I want to try. Or else I wouldn't have met with you.'

'I know.'

'Then what's wrong?'

Carol looked at Niall, rolled her bottom lip between her teeth, and clenched her fingers in her lap.

Lin took a step back. She dropped to a crouch and, even with her knees spread, the huge dressing gown covered every inch of her body from the neck down. 'I'm nervous too. But I like you. Both of you. You're very sexy. Niall is funny and kind. Back home, so few people look like you. Everyone is like me, small and pale.'

Turning back to Lin, Carol saw the earnest intensity in her eyes. 'I'm sexy?' she murmured.

'Extremely.'

'I'll second that, love.'

'Beautiful skin. Big eyes. I like that.'

Carol squirmed on the sofa, shuffling her fingers. 'Thanks, I guess.'

Niall chuckled. 'Hell, she seems more interested in you than me.'

Lin winked. 'Oh, I like you too. But I want to start with Carol. If that's okay?'

'Suits me, love.' With a wide grin, Niall spread his hands.

'I'm asking Carol.'

That made her look up. She stared at Lin, trying to read those dark eyes. They gave nothing away and she wondered just how much of her thoughts lived in her own expression. 'I don't know where to start,' she said. 'I don't normally do girls.'

Lin raised an eyebrow.

'I prefer guys. I messed about with a couple of girls when I was sixteen. But since then, just guys.'

'Then why all this?'

She shrugged. 'Niall and I have been together for nearly ten years.'

'And?'

'She means I'm boring.'

'I don't!' Carol gripped a fistful of her jeans. She stared straight ahead. 'What I mean is, I— no— we wanted something different. A change. Is that so bad?'

'Of course not. But a threesome is a big step.'

'I know.'

'Especially with a woman. So why not a man?'

'Because, no.' Niall broke in. 'Just . . . no.'

Lin chuckled. 'Fine. But this is okay?'

'Two women crawling all over my body? Hell yes!'

'Good.' Standing, Lin took a small step back and unfastened the cord on the dressing gown. She did it slowly with covert glances through her eyelashes.

Carol stiffened. Even she knew the teasing nature of the show was for her benefit. She put her hands in her lap and lifted her gaze high enough to see the robe open.

'Wow.' Niall gave a small groan.

'You like?' Lin whispered.

Tiny knickers, barely more than a strip of red lace and a matching bra with diamante detail.

A lump filled the back of Carol's throat. She swallowed it with effort.

'You're . . .' One hand made a small circle in the air as if to find the answer that way.

'Hot?' Niall offered. 'Freaking sexy?' He bit his lip and slouched deeper into the sofa's embrace, knees spread. His hands lay on his thighs, fingers twitching towards his groin.

Carol closed her eyes. When she opened them again Lin was still there; her beautiful semi-nakedness artfully framed by the blue dressing gown. She stood and wiped her hands on her jeans to clear her sweaty palms.

This close, Carol could look right down on to the top of Lin's head. 'God, you're tiny.'

'I'm five-one.'

'Can you tiptoe or something?'

Lin tilted her head, asking the question with her eyes.

'Kiss me. If I can handle it, we'll go further.'

Lin rose to her toes. Bending to meet her, Carol closed her eyes and touched her lips against those of the smaller woman. 'Did you clean your teeth too?'

'It's only polite.'

Carol brushed her mouth over Lin's one more time. She felt the wet flick of the other woman's tongue and parted her lips just enough to catch a stronger rush of mint and the aftertaste of lager which toothpaste couldn't combat.

Cupping Lin's cheek, Carol held her in place and let her own tongue explore the warm depths.

When the kiss broke, Carol's mouth tingled. Her breath rushed between her lips with a low whistle.

She heard Niall shift on the sofa.

'That's the sexiest thing I've seen all night,' he whispered.

'Really?' Carol asked.

'God, yes. I want to fuck you so badly right now.'

Lin laughed. The sound seemed too big for her tiny body. 'Your Niall is a passionate man.'

Some of the tension lingering in Carol's shoulders finally eased away. A real smile touched her lips and she trailed her fingers down the side of Lin's face. 'I suppose he is. But tonight, let's share him.' With that, she spun around and clambered into Niall's lap.

He grinned and raised his hips, showing off just how pleased he was to have her so close.

She fisted her hands in his hair and used the grip to angle his head for a kiss. Long and slow, the kiss grew into a playful jousting of tongues. The ball of his tongue piercing knocked her teeth, giving the kiss its own percussion.

Never breaking contact, Carol pressed her hips harder into Niall's groin.

His response was to lift her top and play with the bare skin underneath.

Carol felt Lin behind her when the kiss broke, far closer than she'd been a moment ago. Those dainty hands touched her shoulders then stroked down, a tender and intimate massage along her spine.

'Is this okay?' she whispered.

'Yes, go on.'

Lin stepped forward. Her tiny body pressed in and Carol felt soft strands of the other woman's hair tickle the back of her neck.

'Turn around,' Lin whispered.

What Carol lacked in grace she made up in speed as she turned in Niall's lap.

Using firm fingertip-strokes, he continued the massage of her ribs. Those same fingers pulled her down to sit again, and the hard length of Niall through his jeans made Carol wriggle against him.

Lin slipped her hands beneath the top and lifted it several inches. 'You have a nice body. Can I take this off?' She teased one digit up Carol's stomach, then higher, following the same path of Niall's fingers along her ribs.

'Hell yes!' Niall grunted and tried to lift the top himself.

'I'm asking Carol.'

'It's okay. I'll get it.' Carol leaned forward, caught the bottom of the top, and pulled it over her head. She held it for a few awkward moments before Lin tugged it away and let it fall.

Niall ran his hands over her bra, grabbing her breasts to make two handfuls, which he moulded with a playful squeeze. 'She's hot too, right, Lin? Don't you think?'

'Niall!'

Lin moved close enough that her breath whispered over Carol's skin in a quick, hot gust. 'He's right.'

'See?'

'I like breasts.'

The bizarre sensation of being both watched and played with sent a shiver through Carol's body. She abandoned herself to the feel of Niall's fingers and allowed her gaze to fall on Lin. The hunger in the smaller woman's eyes made her grind her legs together.

With deft hands she reached out and pushed the dressing gown off Lin's shoulders. Fluffy blue cloth fell away to leave Lin in just her lacy underwear.

Her small breasts thrust up and out against the cups of her bra, the dark circle of her areola visible along with a glint of silver.

Carol squinted. 'What's that?'

'Where?'

'In your bra.'

'Oh.' Lin grinned and unfastened the bra completely, tossing it over her head.

Niall moaned. 'Wow.' His hands tightened on Carol's breasts. 'Both of them.'

Carol stared at the silver bars running through Lin's nipples. She licked her lips. 'I love piercings,' she murmured.

'I know.' Niall's whisper against her ear held a slight tremble.

Pleasure filled Lin's eyes. 'Touch them if you like.'

A quick glance at the other woman's face reassured Carol that the offer was genuine. Safe in that knowledge, she brushed her fingers against the left piercing. The nipple immediately hardened into a solid pebble of flesh.

Carol bent to touch it with her tongue, running its tip over and around the small point.

Lin closed her eyes. Her head tipped back to expose the line of her throat.

Carol was dimly aware of Niall's hand reaching around her to cup the other breast and play with the piercing.

Her own nipples tingled. She felt them press against the cups of her own boring cotton bra. 'Niall, do mine.'

'Yes, ma'am!'

Carol felt both of his hands at her back and enjoyed the few seconds of Lin's breasts all to herself. Then her bra loosened and joined the growing pile of clothing on the floor.

Beneath her hands, Lin began to squirm; small motions chased by tiny exhalations from parted lips.

Switching to the other piercing, Carol gave it the same lavish attention. She swirled her tongue up. Down. Around. Worried the bar with her teeth. The same moment she bit down, both of Niall's hands cupped her own breasts and squeezed with the rough attention she loved.

She nibbled around Lin's breast and let her hands feel their way down the smaller woman's body. So smooth and soft all over. Like gliding over satin. She stopped at the top of the red knickers and traced the line of Lin's stomach along the top of it.

'I'll take them off.' Lin stooped, easing the lace down her legs at the same time. When she straightened, a neat line of curly hair, previously hidden, marked a tantalising path between her legs. 'What do you think?'

Carol stared.

'You don't like?' For the first time, a hint of uncertainty crept into Lin's voice.

'I'm just remembering my sixteenth birthday.' She looked at Lin and smiled. 'Don't worry, it's a happy memory.'

'Hey, I'm still here, ladies!' Niall pulled Carol against his erection. 'Feel that?' His voice trembled. 'Don't forget me, okay?'

Lin gave a sly wink.

'Sorry.' Carol felt a stab of guilt. She looked at Lin and her beautiful piercings, then back over her shoulder to Niall, his features pinched with need. With a twist of her hips she slid off his lap on to her feet. Then she turned, dropped to her knees and lifted his shirt above the line of his belt. She heard him suck in a sharp breath and enjoyed the tension she could feel through his knees.

Watching his eyes the whole time, she unfastened the belt. Then the button on his jeans. The zip.

When she found the fabric of his boxers, Carol licked her lips. He was so hard. So ready. Struggling to be loose of the cotton.

She pulled him free with one hand and heard an appreciative coo from Lin.

'Big boy,' said the smaller woman.

Niall chuckled and thrust his chest out. 'You know just what to say.'

Carol rolled her eyes and put her mouth around him.

His laughter cut off with a groan.

She sucked him in, controlling the depth and angle with her hands on his hips. Smooth skin, hard flesh, running with bulging veins which gave him the familiar texture she knew and loved. His hairs tickled her nose, filling her nostrils with the scent of musky, roused male. Carol closed her eyes and concentrated on sucking, occasionally pulling back enough to flick her tongue over and around his swollen tip.

'Carol?'

She sucked harder.

'If you keep that up, I'll be the only one who gets any fun.' His breathing hitched.

She dipped a hand into his boxers to massage the twin sacs beneath.

Strain filled his voice. 'Christ, Carol.' A gasp. 'Really, stop a second. Please!'

She leaned back. A long line of saliva joined her mouth to his tip, and she watched the gleaming strand stretch and break before gazing into Niall's reddened face. 'What?'

He gave a shaky laugh. His hands shook as he raised them to his face. 'Have mercy, okay? You know me – I won't last if you do that.'

'I like sucking you off.'

'I know.' Niall raised his hips high enough to remove his jeans and boxers. 'But take it easy. We've got all night.'

Though the sight of her boyfriend naked was one Carol knew well, feeling Lin press against her made it all so much better.

The smaller woman touched Carol's shoulders; a light play over the upper arms before curving around to cup her breasts. Much as Niall had done, Lin squeezed with bold, confident motions which seemed to belong to much larger hands.

'Kiss her neck,' Niall suggested. 'She loves that.'

Lin's lips grazed the side of Carol's throat. A tentative brushstroke, followed by a lingering pass of that small, wet tongue.

Carol shuddered. She cupped her hands over Lin's and held tight until the other woman had to kneel with her. The motion pressed those piercings against her spine, and a spike of pleasure speared Carol's body. She whimpered and spread her knees on the carpet.

'Actually,' Niall whispered, '*this* is the sexiest thing I've ever seen.' He grabbed his stiff length with his left hand and began rubbing, fumbling his shirt buttons with the other. Seconds later a spray of buttons flew through the air.

'Niall!'

He threw the shirt on the floor. 'I don't care, Carol. Fuck, if you could just see yourself.' Naked, he leaned deeper into the sofa and spread his legs. Both hands now; one rubbing, the other squeezing, he worked himself into a hip-bucking frenzy. 'Lin, get those jeans off her. I want to see how wet she is.'

Carol grinned and dropped to all fours, enabling Lin to remove her jeans from behind. She used the time to stare at Niall, to watch him pull and twist and stroke. She became aware of her racing heartbeat and the tingle of lust coursing through her skin. Every nerve ending alive with desire.

He stared back, just as intense, sweat beading on his brow.

The jeans came down her thighs, taking soaking-wet knickers with them.

With a kick and a twist she too was naked, free to crawl back to the sofa and put her mouth around Niall's straining length again.

Lin held up the knickers. 'She's very wet.'

Glancing over her shoulder, Carol saw Lin raise the damp fabric to her face and lick it.

'Wow,' she whispered, 'that *is* sexy.'

Niall hissed and shoved his hands into her hair, guiding her head into a bobbing rhythm.

Next, Lin's hands came into play. A warm palm. A long finger, stroking up then down the slick wetness hidden between Carol's thighs.

She spread her legs wider to let Lin squeeze into the space between them. The other woman now lay on her back beneath her and Carol lifted herself higher on her knees to give her room.

Her body bucked when the tactic between her legs changed. Slender fingers pulled away and, in their place, Lin's tongue took over.

The soft lapping across her labia sent fizzing jolts of pleasure bubbling through Carol's body. The tongue tip wormed deeper, aiming straight for the little nub of her clitoris.

She groaned, a sound that hummed back and forth across her lips and tongue until Niall jerked against the back of her throat, his hips thrusting off the sofa.

'God,' he cried. 'Oh, God.'

Carol lifted her head, gasping for air. Sweat slicked her face and she took a second to wipe it away before whispering, 'Floor.'

Niall slithered off the sofa and on to his knees. Carol would have followed, but Lin's ministrations grew more urgent and two fingers slipped passed Carol's outer lips to caress her insides and scissor their way in and out with powerful strokes. Her tongue continued flicking, lapping, and playing with all the spots Carol often chose to manipulate herself.

She stared at Niall and saw him grin.

'I told you another woman was a good idea.'

'Lie down.'

He shrugged and obeyed, stretching out beside them and rubbing Lin's stomach with a lazy hand. She twisted under his touch and gave a tiny whimper, one that travelled to her tongue and sent the vibration straight through Carol with a pleasurable buzz.

Gasping, she pulled away. It took several seconds to get her breath back and when she did, she crawled up on to the sofa. 'Wow, Lin.'

The smaller woman smiled from her prone position, lips and chin glistening. She shrugged. 'I told you, I like women.'

'And men?'

'Yes, very much.'

'Let Niall eat you while I ride him.'

His eyes widened. 'Are you sure?'

'I want to know if I like watching as much as I remember.'

'You're going to have to tell me more about your adventures before I met you, love.'

'Quick, before I change my mind.' She slithered off the sofa to straddle Niall, teasing him at her slick entrance by jerking up and down each time he angled for entry.

He tried to catch her hips and pull her forward, but Lin grabbed his hands and pressed them to the floor. She put her knees on either side of his head and positioned herself above his face, similarly tormenting him by staying just out of reach.

She looked over her shoulder and caught Carol's gaze. 'He's so eager.'

'You have no idea.'

'Ladies!' Niall's voice cracked. The muscles across his arms and shoulders bunched as he tried to lift his hands, fighting against Lin's weight. When he did free himself, he used them to pinch those twin nipple piercings.

Lin tipped her head back. 'He's making it hard to resist, Carol.'

She grinned. 'Then don't.'

As if it were prearranged, Lin lowered herself on to Niall's mouth the same moment Carol ended her ruthless teasing. She slid forward and angled her hips to allow his whole length to push into her; a single, fierce thrust made smooth by her own excitement.

The penetration sent crests of pleasure rolling through her body and she waited just long enough to regain control of her trembling thighs. Then she rocked her hips, back and forth, round and round, building the rhythm she knew would take her to the end.

Niall's heels drummed the floor. His hands grabbed Lin's hips, and Carol watched him cling to her. The smaller woman pressed her pubis into his face with more of those tiny yelps of pleasure, tangling her fingers in her hair.

Carol rode his bucking hips and leaned back to brace her hands against his knees for a fresh angle. The shift in penetration struck her deep, and she clenched her teeth to keep the shrieks caged in.

She felt the release building in the pit of her stomach; a bud of ecstasy which unfurled like a flower in bloom and blossomed through her body in wave after raging wave.

Niall caught his breath. His thighs tensed. A shudder travelled up his legs.

Seconds later, Niall's release burst from his body in a warm rush filling Carol's body in every sense of the word. He gave a great groan and thrust upwards with his hips, pressing against the deep parts of her that responded best. It took several more thrusts, but moments later she followed him into bliss and let go of his knees to grip her own breasts and pinch her nipples, drawing out the pleasure.

She shuddered her way through a thundering orgasm and saw an impression of gold stars beneath her closed eyelids. Sounds and smells shrank down to nothing, reducing her to a being of pure physical sensation, responding to the lightest touch, the softest breath.

Her skin tingled from forehead to toes, and even the tickle of Niall's hairy legs against her palms added to her pleasure.

Carol returned to her body slowly.

The rest of her senses kicked back into gear one at time. First she heard the dry rasp of her own laboured breathing. Then her nostrils flared, drawing in the unmistakeable musk of recent sex. The sweat on her face dribbled into her mouth and each burst of salt tingled on her tongue.

She slumped forward on her knees and tilted her head just far enough to look around.

Lin had another grin on her face. And a look of fierce hunger in her eyes.

'Fuck,' Niall whispered. 'Holy, holy fuck. I can't breathe.'

'Sorry.' Lin immediately rolled away from him to sit cross-legged near his outstretched arm. 'Are you okay?'

'Oh, yes.'

Carol's body trembled with aftershocks, little jolts reminding her that had been her most intense orgasm in weeks. She tried to move sideways, but even that small motion made Niall twitch inside her. She yelped.

'Don't move yet, please.' He swallowed. 'Give me a second.'

She looked at Lin. 'Did you . . .?'

'Have an orgasm?' She shook her head. 'No, I take time.'

'Niall,' Carol shook her head. 'You could have finished her off.'

He gave her a wide-eyed stare. 'Seriously? How about you try doing so many things at once. Jesus, love, I'm not Superman.'

'It's okay. I still had fun.' Lin pulled her knees up to her chest and wrapped her arms around her shins. 'You are very good. Both of you.'

Niall sighed. 'Thanks.'

Though still buzzing with the afterglow, Carol couldn't help but dart a glance at Lin. She bit her lip. 'I'm really sorry, Lin. Maybe . . . maybe next time you can . . . you know.'

'Next time?' Niall sat up, causing Carol to overbalance.

She grabbed his shoulders and laughed at his startled yelp.

'Don't pinch me. It's too soon.'

'Sorry.' She let go.

He arched an eyebrow. 'Not there, love.'

She grinned and flexed her internal muscles.

'Stop it!'

Chuckling, Carol returned her attention to Lin. 'Next time . . . if that's okay with you?'

Lin nodded. 'Of course. But why wait? I can do it now.' With that, Lin unfurled her arms and reclined on her elbows. She pressed her feet flat to the floor then slid them apart, exposing herself between the frame of her slim thighs. 'You can watch.'

Niall let out a whimper and craned his head to look. 'I'm in heaven,' he whispered. 'This is fucking heaven.'

Carol climbed off him. His semi-stiff flesh slid out of her body with a faint, wet sucking noise and began to rise again. 'Jesus, you're a machine.'

'I'm motivated.' He scrambled up and leaned against the sofa. Grabbing Carol, he pulled her against him and arranged her between his legs so he could fondle her breasts with both eager hands. 'You complaining?'

'No, but—'

'Then shut up and watch the show.'

Relaxed against his chest, Carol watched Lin spread her legs still wider and put one hand between them. One finger vanished inside her, then two, then three and very soon her slender hips bucked and rolled in a near hypnotic dance.

Mouth open, Carol watched and felt the rising warmth in her belly that warned her of an approaching repeat performance. She shifted against Niall's chest. Lifted one of his hands off her breasts and guided it between her own legs to mimic Lin's movements.

He took the hint and slipped two fingers inside her, crooking them forward to catch the sensitive spot which made her legs spasm against the floor.

'Think you can do it again?' he whispered in her ear. 'I'd love to make you come while you watch Lin strum herself.'

Carol grunted. The next orgasm was on its way and the familiar tingle in her toes gained rapid momentum as it rose through her legs. She used her last steady breath to ask, 'What about you?'

'I'm not ready yet. But I will be after this.'

Two feet away, Lin let out a shrill squeal and thrashed against her fingers, twisting one of the silver bars in her nipples with her free hand until her skin stretched pale and taut.

Thrust out over the edge of a second orgasm, Carol closed her eyes and rode Niall's fingers to the end. She felt the heat of Niall's fresh erection press against the small of her back and the tell-tale dribble of moisture from his tip.

Lin's orgasm seemed to last forever, punctuated by little yips and moans that echoed the earlier noises from upstairs.

Carol held Niall's hand in place and pressed it deeper, running her free hand over the rest of her body until the fizzing prickle of physical gratification spread through every inch of her skin.

With a last moan, Lin slumped back and let her fingers fall free of her body. Her chest rose and fell, the silver gleam of her piercings catching the light.

'Better,' she gasped. 'I couldn't have waited for next time.'

Carol crawled away from Niall to get closer to the panting, spread-eagled figure on the floor. She took Lin's limp hand and raised it to her lips, pushing the damp, musky fingers into her mouth one by one.

Niall whimpered. 'When can we see you again, Lin?'

'What he said,' Carol whispered.

Lin gave a shuddering sigh. 'Tuesday? Come to my house.'

'I thought you wanted neutral ground?' Niall wobbled upright. He made it as far as a half crouch before toppling down again. Shrugging, he extended his legs and took his firm length into his hands again.

'For the first time, yes. But since we know this will happen again . . .?' Lin looked at Carol and smiled when she nodded her consent. 'Then please, my house. I have toys.'

'Toys?' Niall's strangled voice made Carol laugh out loud.

'Yes. Toys.' With a slight smile, the woman stood and pulled on the blue dressing gown. 'Think about it. I'm going to check my dress.'

Carol waited for the door to shut behind her before looking back at her boyfriend. She watched him fondle himself then crawled towards him. 'I guess I can close that extra thread on Fetlife asking for a bloke to join us.'

'Wait, what?' He stopped stroking. 'What thread?'

She lifted one shoulder in a lazy half shrug. 'I figured if you could talk me into another girl, I could eventually talk you into another guy. It's only fair.'

'No.' He released himself long enough to grab her by the wrists. He yanked her forward and pressed a hard kiss against her mouth. 'You've got me. You don't need another guy.'

Carol felt the solid edges of his teeth and the lingering flavour of Lin's musk clinging to his lips. 'You sure about that?'

'Yes.'

'Really?' she whispered against his mouth. 'Even if he's just spice?'

He grunted. 'We'll talk about it. Later.' Niall placed a hand on the top of her head and gently pushed down. 'For now. . . I don't think you were finished down here.'

Grinning, Carol allowed him to guide her face down the front of his body.

BILL

Bill closed the Tube8 viewing window when he heard the door open. He smiled as Vicki entered the bedroom. 'Great party, Sis.'

She grinned and stepped forward, arms outstretched.

Slapping the lid shut, he left the laptop and stood to meet her proffered hug. 'You okay?'

'Fine. Just tired.'

'Where's Lara?'

'My room. She's sleeping it off.'

He grinned, ignoring his sister's peevish look. 'Good. She's nicely wasted. Who's downstairs?'

'Carol and her boyfriend. And whoever it was they brought with them.'

'That Asian girl? She was nice.'

Vicki glared. 'You were chasing Simone all night.'

'And?'

'One at a time, Bill.'

'Why? There's enough of me to go around.'

Scandalised, she folded her arms tight enough to make her clothing bunch. 'You're a pig.'

'And you love me anyway.' Eyeing her face, he noticed the red patch of a fresh graze on her left cheek. He jabbed the area with his index finger. 'What happened there?'

She shrugged him away. 'Nothing. Just . . . cut myself.'

'Doing what? Shaving? I warned you about lady razors.'

'Screw you, Bill.' She thumped him on the arm and returned to the door. 'I'm turning in. You okay in here?'

'I'll live.'

'Sorry about the bed.'

He glanced at the collection of sheets folded neatly beside the messy stack of pillows and duvets. 'Yeah; what kind of host are you?'

'A busy one.'

'Wow, chill, Sis. Just kidding. It's a nice place.'

'Thanks. G'night.' She left.

Only when the sound of her footsteps retreated from the door did Bill return to his laptop. He flipped it open and watched it boot while listening to the soft murmur of voices from left-over revellers downstairs.

He considered fetching some water, but quickly decided the trip down the stairs would be too much effort. Instead he reached for the last dregs of his beer and downed the warm liquid while perched on the end of the bed.

He burped. 'Nice.'

After crushing the plastic cup, he tossed it on the floor. His guilt over littering the floor lasted only until he looked around the rest of the box room.

Bare white walls with patches stripped of paint and a threadbare carpet, wardrobe, chest of four drawers and a tiny desk on which his laptop sat.

At least the bed was a double – fine quality, but lacking sheets. The pillow cases stank; fusty and slightly damp like the attic they'd come from. Covered in small clusters of red fluff they looked like fabric chickenpox sufferers.

The laptop returned to the main screen and interrupted his twisted train of thought. He cut an appreciative glance at his desktop photo. 'Just you and me,' he murmured.

The woman on screen was naked, of course, gazing at the camera with big, smoky eyes ringed with too much make-up. She held a cream bun in one hand, positioned halfway towards her heavily rouged lips. The other hand snaked down to nestle between her legs hiding her most private parts.

Not much point in that.

He glanced at his watch, gnawing his bottom lip as he pondered just what he could get away with. 'Can't get any worse . . . .' Pulling his mobile from his pocket, one eye still pinned to the screen, he held down '5' and waited.

The line connected with a click. 'Hello? Who's this?' The voice on the other end sounded wide awake despite the late hour.

'Simone,' Bill chuckled and rolled back on the bed, staring at the ceiling. 'Your best fantasy, baby.'

Silence. Then, 'Bill?'

'How did you know?'

'No one else is that much of an idiot. How the hell did you get my number?'

'Vicki.'

'What— She— I'll kill her!'

'It's not her fault. I made her tell me. Okay . . . I tricked her. She was easy prey. Hello? Simone?'

She sighed. 'What? It's late.'

He gazed at the woman on his laptop and rubbed the front of his jeans. 'You know . . . you've got a very sexy voice.'

'Goodnight, Bill.'

'Wait!'

'Stop being a prick. I want to go to bed.'

It took all the willpower he possessed to bite his lip over the saucy comments creeping into his head. With a deep breath, he paced himself and said, 'I called to apologise. I didn't mean to upset you tonight.'

'Oh.' Some of the venom leaked from Simone's voice. 'Thanks.'

'I'm a nice guy. I just wanted to help.'

'I don't need your help.'

Biting his lip didn't help this time. Before he could think, the words burst free; 'Then why are you chasing Eric like a bitch in heat?'

'He's not gay!'

'Oh, he is, Simone. I'm not making it up. Just ask him, for Christ's sake.'

'You just can't stand the fact that I prefer him. Stop . . . stop making shit up to ease your ego.'

The phone creaked under his grip. 'I'm not! Jesus, if I let him suck my dick would that show you?'

The line clicked and died.

'Hello? Simone?' Bill tossed the mobile on to the bed. 'Bitch! Talk about cock-block.'

Leaping up, he paced the room. Back and forth, over and over, until he tripped on his rucksack. Clothes spilled out, along with his tablet, several DVDs, an MP3 player and a pack of extra-large Durex.

Grunting, he shoved aside three horror flicks and a box set of Indiana Jones in favour of *Liberty Belle's Night Out*, *Roxy's Adventures In Amsterdam* and *Paid In Manhattan*.

After a few seconds of deliberation, he decided on the last of the three titles, grinning at the suggestive cover photo.

The woman depicted looked much like the one on his laptop, though this one was dressed. If one could count a thin coat of flour and a tiny apron as clothing.

'I knew I'd need you,' he murmured, shoving the disc into the laptop.

While the film loaded, he made clumsy attempts to dress the bed. The fitted sheet and pillowcases were easy, but the duvet fought him at every turn until he gave up and tossed the cover on the floor. He sat back down, pulled off his jeans, and spread the bare duvet over his knees.

A soft moan came from the laptop, accompanied by some generic, supposedly sexy, saxophone music.

The film opened to a cheap, badly designed hotel room. In it lounged a man wearing a smoking jacket sitting at a low table, pipe in hand, flicking through a newspaper.

Bill groaned. 'Christ, are you kidding?'

He scrolled through the film, skipping scenes until the maid appeared.

Unlike the cover, this woman was blonde. Her make-up came straight from the Barbie factory and matched her long, French manicured nails and hair extensions.

It would do. Dipping both hands into his boxers, Bill grasped a handful of stiffening flesh and gave it an experimental squeeze.

'Room service, sir. What would you like me to do with your clean sheets?' The woman spoke in a low voice, all sultry and rough. Like a chain smoker.

The man opened his smoking jacket and let it fall. 'Put them right over there. I have a tip for you.' When he stood, it was clear he was totally naked but for a tiny pair of leopard-print pants and more than his fair share of coarse black hair across his chest and stomach.

Bill groaned. 'Fuck me, this is old.'

He heard a thump from outside the bedroom door.

Frozen, Bill listened to the house. He caught the sound of boards settling, the central heating clicking off, and the soft padding of feet on the stairs. He glanced at the film, shrugged and hit pause. That done, he opened the door and peered into the hallway.

He saw a small figure with dark hair walking down the stairs in a blue dressing gown he recognised from the bathroom. 'Vic?'

No answer.

His stomach gave a little flutter when he realised it was probably the small Asian girl Vicki had talked about. Frowning he ducked into the bathroom and saw, soaking in the sink, a small red dress.

He stirred the water with his finger. *Yep, that's her.*

Somewhat disappointed that there was no underwear soaking with the dress he left the bathroom to return to his room.

Halfway there he heard a soft groan. *Now what?*

Creeping towards his sister's room he stopped outside the door. Silence. Bill raised one hand to rap the wood and jumped when he heard the unmistakable shriek of Lara's name. A couple of gasps and a sharp intake of breath. Then a slow whine, the likes of which he recognised from several other choice films in his collection.

'Christ!' He leapt away from the door and fled to his room, slamming the door behind him. Hurling himself on to the unmade bed, he pulled all the pillows over his face and pressed them against his ears.

Though the thick silence of down and goose feathers he imagined he could still hear Vicki's heavy breathing and Lara's laboured gasps.

I guess Malcolm really is out of the picture. He fought back a grin. 'Good.

Tosser,' he added aloud.

Though he tried to stop it, the idea of his little sister tonguing the feisty redhead made him squirm. He thought of Lara's shiny hair, beautiful skin and long legs. A sigh slipped from his mouth. 'Pity she *is* bloody gay.'

Leaving the bed, he returned to the laptop and considered pressing 'play'. On screen the blonde maid was kneeling before the hairy man with her tongue poking from the side of her mouth. Her manicured nails scraped his thighs and left pale lines against his skin. Not sexy in the slightest.

Bill sighed and closed the media player.

'This isn't fair. There's got to be something better than this.'

Only then did he remember the Wi-Fi.

In moments he'd returned to Tube8 and resumed his search of the new releases section.

Since his last visit, several hundred new videos had been posted, though a glance at the thumbnails warned him of the appalling quality.

Just the same he clicked one halfway down and began to watch.

The video opened to show a woman in her late forties. Utterly naked she lay on a threadbare sofa, holding a carrot in one hand and a cucumber in the other.

'No!' He closed the mini-viewing panel. 'Damn you, Simone.' He glared at his abandoned mobile. 'You should be up here now. With your sexy arse and sweet, fuckable mouth.'

He found another video. Thank God. It's pretty difficult to fuck up a blow job.

And so it was. The video ended ten minutes later with the obligatory cum shot and the display of creamy-white fluid on the end of an overworked tongue.

The scene finished before he felt more than a twinge of pleasure in his own cock, the flesh barely at half mast. He groaned, tucked himself back into his boxers, and added a sigh for good measure. 'Wow. Boring as fuck.'

A small ping issued from the laptop speakers, followed by a small Skype pop-up window in the bottom right corner.

HIRAL CALLING

Bill opened the conversation window.

HIRAL_6943 SAYS: HEY B, U CHATTIN?

He grinned, sat down and angled himself for a better typing position.

BILL-I-ARD BALL SAYS: U SHLD B IN BED

HIRAL_6943 SAYS: CNT SLEEP. HORNY. U CHATTIN?

BILL-I-ARD BALL SAYS: AM NOW

HIRAL_6943 SAYS: GOOD.

The window disappeared, replaced by a small yes-no dialogue box.

HIRAL WANTS TO START A WEBCAM CONVERSATION WITH YOU. CONFIRM: YES? NO?

After checking the volume on his speakers, Bill clicked 'yes'.

On screen he caught sight of Hiral. She was at home from what he could tell, wrapped in a silky dressing gown so sheer it was almost pointless. He could see the lines of her night dress beneath and the plump points of her nipples a little lower down.

He licked his lips. 'Um, Hiral . . . what are you wearing?'

She frowned. 'A nightdress.'

'Don't you think it's a bit . . . you know?'

'Pervert. It isn't for you. I have a friend coming over when he finishes work. It's for him.'

'Oh. A friend. Nice.' He scratched the back of his neck. 'Do I know him?'

'No.' She pulled tighter on the dressing gown and shook her head until long dark hair fell into her eyes. 'How was the party?'

'Great. Seems like Vicki had a really good time. Still is from what I can tell.' He snorted. 'All right for some.'

'Aww, poor baby.' Hiral pushed her lips into a pout. 'Did poor little Billy-Willy not pull tonight?'

He sucked his teeth. 'No actually. Simone spent the whole night chasing Eric. Refused to believe he's a fucking fudge packer. Christ's sake.'

'You saw Simone?'

He nodded.

'I didn't know she was going.'

'I think she'd been somewhere else first, she looked too fucking hot for a house party. Tiny dress, legs all the way up there,' he gestured to beyond head height. 'Fantastic tits.' The image made him groan. 'What a cock-tease.'

'Maybe she's just not interested. Believe it or not, you're not all that.'

Bill glared. 'I don't remember you ever complaining.'

'Until I dumped your arse.'

'Is this why you wanted to talk to me? To rub salt in the wounds? Fuck, if I want torture, I'll watch *Strictly*, thanks. I'm going to bed.' He reached out to sever the connection, jerking his hand back when Hiral shrieked at him.

'No, wait!'

'What?' he snapped. 'I'm not in the mood.'

She bit her lip and played with her fingers; a curious dry-washing motion Bill usually associated with scolded children. 'Sorry I— this isn't what I wanted.'

'What *did* you bloody want, then?'

Hiral looked away. When she looked back two wet tracks glistened on her cheeks.

Bill gaped. 'What the hell, woman? What's wrong with you?'

'I made a mistake.'

'What?'

'Dumping you. It was a mistake.'

He rubbed his face with both hands. After staring at the floor for a moment or two, Bill took a deep breath and looked back at the screen. 'Okay . . .?'

'What the fuck— Is that all you've got? "Okay"?'

'What do you want me to say? You dump me – over the phone by the way! – then spend the next two weeks letting me know how many of your friends have been over.' He put air quotes around 'friends' and gritted his teeth. 'By all accounts you've sucked more cock in the last two weeks than you ever did the whole three years we were together.'

Hiral leaned right up to the camera. Her face loomed large in the display window until Bill could count the individual lashes framing her big brown eyes. 'You dumb shit,' she snapped. 'Are you really that dense?'

'What?'

'There *is* no friend. There never has been.'

He opened his mouth. Closed it. Waved his hand in a 'well?' gesture.

'I was trying to make you jealous.' She tangled her fingers in her hair and pulled. 'God, you're so annoying.'

'What have I done now?'

'Nothing. Just— Nothing.'

Bill stared at her. 'So . . . no guys?'

'No.'

'No dirty threesome with strap-ons and whips?'

'Did you actually believe that?'

He thought about it. 'Not really. But it sounded good.'

She laughed. Wiped the tears from her plump coffee-coloured cheeks. 'Sorry. I wanted you to be jealous.'

'Why?'

The laughter faded. 'Because I made a mistake. I shouldn't have dumped you. It was stupid. And it's not like I don't occasionally check out other guys too. I miss you.'

He stared at the screen.

'Aren't you going to say anything?'

'No— I mean yes. Fuck, Hiral. It worked.'

'What did?'

'The jealousy thing. Why do you think I was chasing that skinny bimbo, Simone? I don't even like blondes. And she's built like a broomstick, no curves or anything.'

Hiral's laugh was warmer this time. 'I used to call you a chubby chaser.'

'You're not chubby. You're perfect. Great smile. Beautiful hair. Amazing tits. And the best cock-sucking skills I've ever come across in my life.'

'Bill!'

'It's true. No one has ever sucked me off like you used to. Hand on heart.'

'Thanks. I guess.'

He gazed at the screen. 'What now?'

Hiral shrugged. Then bit her lower lip. 'Seems a shame for me to get all dressed up and not take advantage of it.' She shimmied her shoulders until the sides of the dressing gown slipped away.

Bill's breath caught in his throat. He gazed at the vast expanse of chest visible above the lacy neckline and the dark shadow formed by her substantial cleavage. 'What are you doing?'

'Watch.' She teased her fingers beneath the straps of her gown and eased them down. It took additional effort to pull the fabric over her heavy breasts but she did it; slow and teasing. Her nipples slipped into view: big, plump and dark against the rest of her skin.

Once more Bill felt a stirring in his boxers and fought the urge to put his hand there. Instead he gripped his thighs and watched Hiral lift her breasts one by one and slurp her nipples into her mouth.

'Bet Simone couldn't do this, right?' She grinned, still circling her left nipple with the very tip of her long pink tongue.

'Probably not.'

'She has tiny boobs. There's no way she could do this.'

Bill shrugged. 'I don't know. I don't care. Just— Keep doing that.'

A giggle slipped out of Hiral's mouth. She stood up and kicked her chair aside, moving into the space it had occupied to show off the rest of her underwear. Black. Lacy. A line of fluffy black fur along the top.

'Show me,' he whispered.

'What?' Hiral cocked her head, a look of unconvincing innocence on her face.

He grinned. He couldn't help it. 'Show me your pussy.'

'Oh, you don't want to see that.'

'Christ, yes, I do.'

'Say please.'

'Please!'

'Please what?'

'Please, Hiral, show me your fucking pussy.'

Smirking, she tugged off the underwear and kicked it to one side. She stood before the webcam naked, showing off every glorious bump and curve.

Bill groaned low in his throat. 'You're so beautiful. Look at you – smooth as a peach too. What happened to the landing strip?'

She shrugged. 'Maintenance.'

'Well that is beautiful. I prefer it.'

'I thought you might.' She reached down, slipping two fingers past her outer lips. The clear, slippery droplets of her excitement were already visible and slid down her knuckles until they glistened in the light.

After fingering herself for a few agonising seconds, Hiral lifted both digits and stuffed them into her mouth. 'You like that?' she whispered.

He nodded. It was all he could manage. Then, with much effort, he stuttered, 'But . . . what does this mean? I don't get it.'

'Can't you just enjoy it?'

'Yes, but . . . .' Bill tried to cover his re-emerging erection.

'Then just watch. Play with me.'

'But I don't get what's happening?'

She sighed. 'Close your eyes.'

'But you just said watch. I can't—'

'Close your eyes, Bill. Trust me.'

After a quick glance at the door Bill did as he was told.

'Good.' Without a visual cue from the laptop, Hiral's voice seemed detached and distant.

Straining to hear it, Bill lowered his breathing and held perfectly still.

'Hold your cock.'

'What?' His eyes flashed open. 'I don't understand what you're—'

'Damn it, Bill! Just grab your fucking cock, close your eyes, and listen to my voice.'

He jumped and, without further questions, wrapped both hands around his stiffening length. 'There,' he snapped, 'happy?'

'Yes actually. But just one hand. Leave the other one free.'

'Any preferences?'

'Don't be a bitch. And use your left hand.'

'Fine.' Bill let the right hand rest on his knee. 'When did you get so bossy?'

'I've always been bossy.'

'You haven't.'

'Then you haven't been paying attention.'

'Now what?'

'I want you to listen to my voice. Really listen. Don't open your eyes until I tell you. Can you manage that?'

'Sure.' Bemusement with an edge of curiosity coaxed Bill into doing as instructed. With his feet flat on the floor, warm member clasped tight in his left hand, he waited.

His body tingled, small hairs rising in the cool air. He heard the faintest murmur of voices below him and his own low breathing. A lick of his lips brought a memory of his last beer to mind, each of his senses working overtime to compensate for the lack of sight.

'I loved the time we used to spend together, Bill. With Vicki and Malcolm before that went to shit. You'd hold my hand, kiss me and always made me feel good.'

'Why did you dump me then?'

'Shut up!' She took a deep breath and continued, 'I remember when we went to Skegness. We left the others on the beach and ran off to one of the arcades. Do you remember? You took me to a storage room and fucked me on the base of one of those safari simulators.'

Bill grinned.

His left hand tightened on the stiffness of his growing erection sliding up, then down. 'We nearly got caught by security.'

'That's right. You left my knickers sticking out of the coin slot.'

Laughter spilled from his mouth. 'Yep. And I had my hand under your skirt the whole drive home. You were so fucking wet, it was amazing. You nearly crashed us into a postbox.'

'You made me come right there in the car. Remember? With Vicki and Malcolm following us on the main road. Then you did it again when we got on to the motorway.'

For a moment Bill couldn't speak. He nodded instead and worked his left hand more urgently inside his boxers. A slick of moisture dampened his fingers and he used it to lubricate his motions.

'My car stank of sex for two weeks afterwards. I still can't sit on that seat without thinking of your fingers inside me. Last Monday I just sat in the car and fingered myself on the driveway. Best orgasm for weeks.'

For the first time Bill became aware of the weight in Hiral's breathing. She gasped and he heard her give a little whimper.

'What are you doing?'

'Keep your eyes closed,' she whispered. 'Put your right hand on your balls.'

This time Bill didn't argue. At once he grasped for his testicles and squeezed. The delicious pressure from his own fingers made him moan and rub more urgently with his left hand. Tiny beads of sweat prickled his brow.

'I miss it, Bill. I miss us being together. I miss the way you touched me and kissed me. You'd bite my neck, I loved that. All those little marks you left behind.'

Bill groaned. 'I liked marking you. It made me feel like you were mine.'

'I was.'

His erection, now hot and trembling, pressed against his boxers. He tugged them down and off, easing the sticky flesh into the open. He tightened his grip and alternated a gentle squeezing motion with a slow caress. His warm sacs grew tight and the dual attention around his groin sent little shivers rushing up and down his spine. Behind his closed eyelids

Bill saw swirls of deep green and purple in the darkness.

Hiral began panting. Soft at first, then harder and the sounds were joined by a wet squelch which Bill knew and recognised.

His eyes popped open before he could help it.

On screen Hiral sat on the chair once more with three fingers buried inside her; sliding in and out at a frantic pace, her eyes, squeezed tightly shut. The other hand fastened on her left breast, pinching and twisting the nipple until it grew dark and swollen. 'Do you remember,' she gasped, 'the last time we slept together? At my house. My parents were downstairs and you went down on me.'

'Best sixty-nine of my life,' he panted, gaze glued to her busy fingers. 'You don't even have a gag reflex any more, do you?'

The squelching noises grew louder as Hiral added yet another finger. Her thumb flicked over her clit and fine trembles rippled down her arms and legs. 'No. I don't need it. Not for you. I never held anything back from you. Not when I was pissed off of course, but not when I was happy either. You got everything.'

Bill timed his hands to move in tandem with Hiral's. For each wet squish of her fingers he jerked on his trembling length, aware of the familiar pressure building in his stomach. He heard Hiral's voice as if from far away, but for the very first time really heard her.

Again he closed his eyes. Listened to her words, her voice as she reminisced about old times and naughty encounters.

Once more without the visual, he relied wholly on his ability to hear and the wet insertion of her fingers over and over seemed louder than ever. He heard the strain in her breathing and the faint guttural grunt as she came closer to orgasm.

'Eyes still closed?' she said.

He hesitated. 'They are now.'

Hiral laughed. 'At least you're honest. You've changed. Still having fun?'

'God, yes.'

'Good. Now let go of your balls and put a finger in your arse.'

'What?'

'You heard me.'

Resisting the temptation to open his eyes, Bill leaned back on his chair. 'I'm not sure.'

'Trust me. You'll like it.'

'I like doing it to *you*.'

'Then believe me . . . you'll like it. Give it a try. For me?'

With everything else wound up so tightly Bill couldn't resist for long. The pressure in his balls was almost unbearable and sweat poured in a near constant stream down his face and back. 'What do I do?'

'What do you do to me?'

Bill thought it through. 'I dip my fingers in your pussy first. You're always wet enough— it's easy.'

'Lick your fingers then. Don't make me do all the work.'

Though it seemed ridiculous, Bill popped his index finger into his mouth and lathered it with saliva. Only when the digit slipped easily between his lips did he remove it. 'I feel weird.'

'Don't. Believe me, this is so sexy.'

'Oh, so you can have your eyes open?'

'Just lie down where I can see you. Put your feet on the mattress. Bend your knees.'

Though he had to open his eyes for this step, Bill was quick to close them again once he reached the bed and flopped into position. He grasped his cock. The press of veins against his fingers heightened his pleasure. Being blind only made it better.

Slippery. Hot. Solid.

Gathering warm droplets from his quivering tip he smeared them all over his skin.

He moved more musky moisture to his other hand and pressed the tip of his finger against the tight hole of his back passage.

'Go on. Do it.' The breathy note returned to Hiral's voice and a low buzz filled the air. 'Trust me.'

Bill's imagination plunged into overload. He saw a vibrator in his mind's eye; pink and textured, the sides slick with Hiral's juice as she pumped it in and out of her body. He saw her mouth wrapped around him, nose buried in his pubic hair, her eyes open, gazing into his as he thrust his hips towards her face. Back and forth, again and again into the delicious warmth of her sexy mouth. He could almost feel her tongue, lashing the underside of his erection, working lower and lower towards that tiny patch of skin behind his balls that she loved to stroke with teasing fingers.

He pushed harder with his finger, fighting the resistance until it popped past the ring of muscle and into the tightness beyond.

A groan spilled out of his mouth.

The sensation was foreign to him, but so pleasurable that his hips jerked forward off the bed, allowing him to push harder. Deeper.

Hiral squealed. It was the first of the sounds which usually signalled the onslaught of a powerful orgasm.

Bill knew it, recognised it, and knew in that moment that he couldn't hold back any longer. He didn't want to.

His left hand pumped harder; a furious pace that bumped his fist against his stomach. He felt the slap of his testicles against the fingers of his other hand and pushed the intruding finger deeper still.

Feet spasming against the bed, he scrunched his eyes shut and let his mouth fall open. Another moan, deeper this time. Longer, and with it a release which made his head spin and feet slap against the bed.

His pleasure gushed over his fingers in a hot, sticky torrent, running down the back of his hand, across his wrist, and on to the bare duvet he'd neglected to cover.

Through the haze of his own release he heard Hiral shriek and the wet pounding of flesh on flesh. The buzzing sound grew louder and a final keening moan signalled Hiral's own orgasm.

Bill's eyes flew open just in time to see her fall sideways off the chair, fingers still thrust firmly inside her. The vibrator hummed through the gush of wetness she released and took on a thick, bubbling pitch.

'Damn, Hiral.' He swallowed, trying to moisten his dry lips. 'You okay? Say something!'

A raised thumb appeared in the bottom half of the screen.

Easing the finger out of his back passage brought on another wave of pleasure he didn't expect. Not quite so much as to bring on another orgasm, but enough that he shuddered and closed his eyes for a moment. His sensitive shaft still stood out straight before him, only slightly relaxed from the release.

Rubbing both hands against the duvet he sat up.

'God, that was . . .'

Hiral reappeared from the bottom of the screen, pushing tousled hair from her face and clicking off the vibrator. 'I told you to trust me.'

'I'll remember. For the future. If . . . you know . . . we're back.'

She gave him a wicked grin. 'Sure. Come over.'

'Really?'

'Yes. Come now. Do that with me for real.'

He reached towards the screen, then changed his mind and wiped his fingers on the duvet again. 'Are you sure? It's really late now.'

'Yes, I'm sure! Come on, Bill! There's spunk all over your sheets anyway; you can't sleep there now. I'll leave the door open for you.'

He grinned. 'Give me half an hour. Keep your vibrator going.' Bill slapped his laptop closed and got dressed.

ERIC & MORGAN

Eric began the third scrub of his hands just as the light clicked on above him.

'Why are you washing up in the dark?' Morgan stood in the kitchen doorway, one hand still resting on the light switch.

'Sorry, did I wake you?' Eric wiped his wrinkly fingers on a tea towel.

'No, I was waiting for you. What are you doing?'

'I smell like lager and junk food. I feel dirty.'

'You don't look it.' Grinning, Morgan walked further into the room and leaned against the table. He tucked a curly wisp of hair behind his ear and folded his arms. 'How was the party?'

'Shitty. I wish you'd been there.'

'Sorry, work reports. But they're done now. I'm all yours.'

Eric glanced at the clock. 'It's nearly 2 a.m. Bit late now.'

'What happened? You're being weird.'

'I just want to go to bed.'

'Talk to me first?'

Eric sighed.

'Come on.' Leaving the table, Morgan put his arms around him.

Eric felt the warmth of his touch through his thin T-shirt and sighed. Morgan's hairy skin and coconut oil scent did much to dampen the lingering effect of the party. He butted his head against the taller man's shoulder. 'I hate going to those things alone.'

'But I bet Niall was glad to see you.'

He nodded. 'But I don't know why he invited me. He was arguing with Carol again.'

'What was it this time?'

'Hell if I know. I kept out of it.'

Morgan stared. 'That's not what's bothering you.'

'No . . .'

'So tell me, already. Then I'll take you to bed.'

'Simone.' Eric wiped his face again and caught the persistent smell of pizza mingled with lemon washing up liquid. 'The one from your office.'

'The Glamo-Bimbo?' Morgan pulled away. 'I didn't know she was going. Who invited her?'

'Bill, I suppose. Chasing muff like always.'

'But what happened?'

Eric bit his lip. 'She rode my back all night.' Now the words were out, Eric couldn't stop them. He tugged free of Morgan's arms and sat in one of the hard-backed chairs surrounding the table. Elbows on the surface, he lowered his face to his hands and spoke through his fingers. 'It felt like she was in heat. Bill flirted like a mo-fo but she wouldn't have it. All fucking night. And she just got more and more wasted. All night, like trying to fend off an octopus with tits. A *drunk* octopus with tits.'

'She does have a lot of tits.' Morgan yawned.

Eric's rant morphed into a snort of laughter. 'Dude, you're not that gay.'

'No, I mean, she's boob-heavy. She's a big girl, right?'

'Only compared to the rest of her. She's like a rake with two oranges strapped to the front.'

'Oranges? You mean melons, right?' Taking the seat nearby, Morgan planted a kiss on the side of Eric's face. 'What did she actually do?'

Eric looked at the floor.

'It can't be that bad.'

'She cornered me in the bathroom. Couldn't even take a piss without her stalking me. When I tried to get out she shoved me in the bath and yanked her dress off.'

Morgan arched an eyebrow. 'Wow.'

'I know, right?'

'Wait until Monday. She's going to regret ever knowing me.'

'I just want to forget it.'

'I can't tease her?' He prodded a knot of loose wood on the table top. 'Clearly she doesn't realise you're gay. Or with me. I could have so much fun with this when I get into the office. I'll make her squirm right out of those cheap Primani heels.'

Eric shook his head. 'No, please. Just leave it.'

'Fine. She stripped in the bathroom. Then?'

'You want all the details?'

'I need to know how upset I should be.'

Palming his face, Eric cut a weary glance at his lover through his fingers. 'She took off the dress but couldn't figure out how the bra worked. While she messed about with that, I bolted and wedged myself between Niall and Carol.'

'And that was better?'

'Hell yes. Even with them bitching at each other. Better than being alone. The stragglers get picked off, you know that.'

'Pussy.'

Eric grunted and punched Morgan in the arm.

'Come on, it's funny. I wish I'd been there to see it. You have no idea how to deal with flirts.'

'I can handle you.'

'Only just. I bet she couldn't stop touching you either. Those manicured talons all over you.'

A frown teased Eric's brow. He looked again at his lover and saw a hint of anger there. 'Nothing happened.'

'I know, but . . . it doesn't matter.' He stood. 'Come to bed.'

Eric stared at Morgan's cheery face, the sexy tumble of his hair. Though he had to hide a yawn behind his hand he felt a little pulse of warmth writhe through his gut.

How did he always manage to look so good?

'Give me a minute, okay? I still feel gross.'

Morgan leaned close.

Eric felt the rush of breath against his ear and the gentle heat of Morgan's body through two layers of clothing. His fingers strayed of their own accord, running through those deep, chocolate-coloured curls and pulling on them.

An answering groan rumbled through Morgan's chest. 'Sure,' he whispered. 'But don't take too long.' After pulling back slowly, he walked away.

In the calm that followed Eric sighed and worked some of the tension out of his shoulders. The buzz of the fridge warred with the rhythmic plinking of the leaking tap above the sink. He rubbed his mouth again, shrinking away from the memory of Simone's clutching fingers. Not for the first time, he wondered how anybody could stand getting quite so drunk. Leaving the sink, Eric kicked off his shoes and followed the smell of coconut oil that seemed to lead the way like an invisible ribbon through the air.

The bedroom, when he reached it, was lit by flickering candlelight. Shadows danced up and down the walls as he approached, and yet it was the sight on the bed that made Eric pause. That warmth in his belly began to spread, and he gnawed on his bottom lip.

Reclined against the pillows, Morgan held up a pair of shot glasses. He was naked but for the play of light across his chest and legs. One hand rested on his cock, hiding it from view. On the sheets near his ribs lay a bowl of strawberries, and on the other side, a small pot of cream.

Eric grinned and leaned in the doorway. 'I thought you said it was late.'

His lover arched an eyebrow. 'I thought you'd be back sooner.'

'What if I'm tired? What if I want to go to bed?'

'Tough,' he shot back. 'I've been working all night while you ran off to parties to have people throw themselves all over your sexy bod. My turn now.'

Moisture filled Eric's mouth, forcing him to swallow it away. He stiffened and ducked his chin. 'I didn't ask for it, you know.'

'Christ, I'm joking. Come here, please.'

He inched closer.

Morgan grinned at him. 'Your ears are all red.'

Ignoring the jibe, Eric unbuttoned his shirt. 'I *am* tired, you know.'

'We'll sleep in. Sunday tomorrow.'

'Football practice?'

'We'll skip it. Unless you prefer football to this.' Morgan lifted the hand covering his groin. Beneath it lay a large mound of whipped cream, topped by two strawberry halves.

Eric bit back a snort of laughter and licked his lips. 'Bastard. I love strawberries.'

'Yep.'

'And cream.' Another step closer.

'I know.'

'Okay. So . . . a few strawberries. Then what?'

'Nothing.' Morgan twisted his hips from side to side. Candlelight caught his eyes and gave them a mischievous glint. 'We eat them, clean our teeth and go to bed.'

'Really?'

'If that's what you want.'

Aware of Morgan's gaze on him, Eric made a show of removing his shirt. Over one shoulder, then the other, he let the garment catch briefly on his elbows before it fell. It pooled on the ground and he stepped over it while unlooping his belt.

When he played his fingers over the zip of his jeans he saw Morgan's mound of whipped cream begin to rise.

Eric grinned. With one hand, then the other, he stroked his chest, teasing briefly over his nipples before leaving the jeans to join his shirt.

With the loss of each piece of clothing the hungry look in Morgan's eyes intensified.

'So,' Eric toyed with the waistband of his boxers, 'just the strawberries? Right?'

'Yes.' Morgan's voice strained around that single syllable.

'Yeah, right.' Boxers off.

Eric crossed the rest of the room naked and stretched out on the bed beside Morgan. His fingers dabbled over the fine spirals of hair dotting that wide, strong chest.

Practically purring under the attention, Morgan plucked a strawberry from the bowl, dipped it in the cream, then held it out.

Holding eye contact, Eric closed his mouth over the flesh of the fruit and clicked his teeth together near the stem.

The explosion of sweetened cream versus the tart tang of strawberry made him shudder. 'Very nice.'

Morgan repeated the process: plucking a strawberry, dipping it, offering it.

This time, Eric allowed his lips to brush Morgan's fingers.

He felt the hard smoothness of the fingernails against his tongue and heard the click as they knocked his teeth.

Gentle but firm, he caught the intruding index finger between his teeth and lathered his tongue around it. The digit tasted wonderful, a sensual mix of fruit and the unique flavour that was all Morgan. Only after thoroughly licking the finger did he let it go, enjoying the deep breaths and wide eyes Morgan gave him in return.

'Tease,' the other man whispered.

'You started it.' A quick shimmy down the bed put Eric's face level with the mound of cream melting between Morgan's legs. He watched runnels of white slide free and run down his thighs, a wriggling path around the curly hair there.

'Getting hot, are you?'

Morgan made a sound between a groan and a whine. 'What the hell do you think? Do something, will you?'

'Something? Something like this?' Eric trailed his fingers over his lover's thighs.

Though he enjoyed the brush of hair against his fingers and the soft sighs in return, he took great care to avoid the cream.

'Or like this?' The next teasing touch was a kiss, brushing his lips against the skin surrounding the cream.

Eric grinned when he felt Morgan flex his stomach muscles.

The whole time he held eye contact, allowing his feelings to pour through the window of his eyes. Answering messages came through Morgan's gaze, coupled with the shift of his thighs and the twitch of his fingers.

Morgan's quick, shallow breaths made his own pulse quicken until he imagined he could hear it thudding in his ears.

His muscles clenched, each brush of skin or hair working to heighten his growing lust.

To continue the tease, Eric leaned forward and lapped up one of the strawberries from the pair nestled in the whipped cream. A lump of cream followed and he saw, in the gap left behind, a small patch of skin.

'These are great,' he murmured. 'Want one?'

'No.' Morgan's voice shook again. 'You have them.'

'Sure?'

'Positive. I want to watch you.'

The words and the grin that went with them sent a shudder rippling down Eric's spine. He lowered his head and nipped at the second strawberry half, making another hole in the modesty coating of cream.

'Get on with it. Please. It's going to make a mess.'

Unbidden, a smile crept on to Eric's face. 'This was your idea,' he cried, leaning back and away from the cream. Ignoring the whispered protests, he crawled back up the bed and level with Morgan's face. 'Your wonderful, genius idea. And I plan to take full advantage.' The kiss he laid on his lover was deep, long and sensual. He kissed Morgan as if seeking hidden treasures in his mouth, exploring every nook, crevice and niche with his tongue. He drank in the delicious taste of him and swallowed every contented murmur which followed.

A bead of sweat slid down the side of Morgan's nose. It slipped down his cheek and pooled in the corner of his delectable mouth. Eric couldn't resist licking it away. 'You taste like cream,' he said. 'Yes . . . sweet, tasty, supposed-to-be-for-me cream. Who said you could eat my treat?'

'My treat too, Eric. Remember, I was working? You were partying?'

'I need it more than you. I've had a traumatic night.' With that, he claimed another kiss.

He groaned as Morgan's hands slid over his body. His shoulders tightened then relaxed beneath the strong pressure of fingers on his shoulders. When Morgan opened his mouth, Eric got another taste of cream followed by more of that sexy Morgan flavour. Like chocolate and honey and spiced fruits, and all the things Eric loved most.

Eventually Morgan drew back. Eric tried to follow, but his lover grabbed his hand and tugged it towards his groin.

'I can't stay like this all night,' he whispered. 'You really need to finish that.'

In answer, Eric turned on the bed and sat backwards astride Morgan's chest, leaning forward until his nose hovered a mere inch above the white expanse of melting cream.

The position put his cock directly in line with Morgan's hot mouth and, seconds later, he felt the whisper of his breath against the sensitive skin. He groaned and shifted his weight as his cock rose, bumping Morgan's chin and catching there. Stubble scraped his sensitive tip.

When the first touch of a slick wet tongue touched his glans he hissed and bit his lip. 'Hey, don't distract me.'

'If you're going to shove your dick in my face I'm going to taste it, Eric.'

'You're spoiling my treat.'

'Not my treat.'

The next lick made Eric grind down with his hips. 'Do you want me to get cream all over the sheets?'

Morgan grunted and stopped licking. 'Christ, you know me far too well.'

'I hope so.' Chuckling, Eric returned to eating.

He started in the creases of Morgan's thighs, lapping up the run-off with long cat-like licks. Next, the skin beneath his belly button until a long line of white stood out starkly against his lover's darker skin.

Eric paused long enough to observe the smooth span of skin beneath him before slurping up the rest with one long swallow.

Gasping, Morgan rocked his hips off the bed, then steadied himself.

'I love how hot your mouth is,' he moaned.

In answer, Eric hummed on his mouthful of cock. He let the sound rumble along his tongue and tightened his lips to make a seal around that stiff, sticky flesh. Another puff of air caressed his balls as his lover exhaled beneath him.

'Harder.' The begging note in his voice left Eric no choice but to obey.

Another suck and the last traces of cream gave way to the taste of his lover's body.

Eric closed his own eyes and stroked both hands up and down Morgan's legs. Rough hair scratched his palms in pleasurable contrast to the smoother skin against his ribs and hips.

Now teeth: soft pressure until Morgan jerked and twisted his hips. His legs trembled and Eric recognised the signs of approaching orgasm.

'Hey.' He pulled his mouth away and shifted to sit on one side. 'Don't you dare come yet, I want you inside me when you do.'

Chest heaving, Morgan slowly cracked his eyes open. He sat up and leaned on his elbows. 'Actually . . . I had an idea about that.' He slipped one hand beneath the pillow and pulled out a tube of lube, a single disposable glove and a bright blue square of shiny foil. 'Here.' He threw them.

Eric allowed himself a small grin as he caught them. 'Bloody boy scout.'

The shiny material crackled against his tongue as he placed a corner between his teeth and pulled. When he reached for Morgan's cock, the other man slithered away up the bed.

'No, no.' As Morgan shimmied away he knocked the bowl of strawberries. Small red fruits littered the rumpled duvet. 'Not me, you.'

'What?'

'It's for you.'

Eric blinked at his fingers and the condom dangling from his grip. He saw the serious look in Morgan's eyes. 'Seriously?'

'Yep.'

'But we don't—'

Morgan frowned. 'Just a suggestion. I thought you might like to try . . .'

Eric couldn't help staring. His insides squirmed, a peculiar mix of confusion, pleasure and fear. He licked his lips and stretched the condom between his fingers. 'You— After Aaron, I just thought . . .' The words faded away. He lowered his head but through his lashes he saw Morgan scoot forward again. Then light fingers, smelling of coconut oil, touched his cheek.

'You're not Aaron. He was a dick. You're not. You won't hurt me. But if you don't want to . . .'

The thudding in Eric's chest kicked up a notch. 'Of course I want to. Bottoming is all well and good but feeling you underneath me . . . Fuck, I'm as hard as a steel rod right now.'

Morgan's face brightened. 'Really?'

'Yes. Feel.' Quick and forceful, Eric grabbed his hand and shoved it between his legs. His cock sprang forward in response. When Morgan's fingers closed over his thick, stiff meat, Eric fought back a groan.

'Just thinking about it,' he murmured, twitching beneath Morgan's skilled grip. He felt the pressure gathering in his balls and sucked in a deep breath. 'Don't . . . quick, let go or it's all over for tonight.' He squirmed. 'Let go!'

Grinning, Morgan gave him one last squeeze and let go. With a smirk he shoved some strawberries out of the way and lay back. 'Good. Lube up. And go slow.'

It took several seconds of deep breathing and thoughts of gardening, tits and shoe shopping before Eric calmed down enough to touch himself. He grasped his stiff length and rolled the condom over it, watching those soft brown eyes the whole time.

The latex hugged his flesh and the faint ribbing on the surface stroked his palms. His tip quivered and brushed his stomach.

Before him, Morgan raised his knees to his chest.

The tiny pucker of his arse winked like a single cheeky eye and Eric stared at the barely there opening, wondering how he would ever fit.

'Hey,' Morgan clicked his fingers. 'Earth to Eric.'

He looked up. 'Sorry, I— sorry.'

'I get it. I'm a bit scared too. Hurry up before I lose my nerve.'

Hands trembling, Eric retrieved the lube and filled his palm with a generous squirt. Cool, slick jelly began to run and slither through his fingers. He rubbed his sheathed cock. 'Fuck! Do you keep this stuff in the fridge?'

More rubbing and thoughts of what would follow brought warmth back to his flesh. He closed his eyes and pumped a few more strokes. A low cough from Morgan brought him back.

'Hot as that is to watch, this isn't a solo flight. Get over here.'

'Sorry.' Eric crawled over the bed, shoving aside mashed up

strawberries. On his way he heard a clunk and, seconds later, his left hand sank into the bowl of cream. 'Fuck . . .'

'Don't worry about it.'

'But the sheets—'

'Come here!' Morgan snaked out a hand and grabbed his wrist, yanking him the rest of the way across the bed. They fell together, Eric on top, positioned just right to see the flicker of surprise in his boyfriend's expression.

'What?' he whispered.

Morgan winced. 'I'm lying on the strawberries. Don't worry about it. Give me your hand.'

Obediently, Eric held out his cream-drenched fingers.

One at a time, Morgan slurped the digits into his mouth and ran his tongue around them.

The hot swirl of that flexible muscle almost made Eric come then and there. Instead, he focused on holding off, knowing there was so much more to follow.

A gust through the open window made the candles gutter and Eric smiled through the dancing shadows. 'You do that so well,' he murmured.

'And you taste amazing.'

Eric swallowed the lump of excitement wedged in the back of his throat. 'I can't stand it. Lift your legs. Turn over. Let me start.'

Without a word, Morgan did as instructed, flipping on the sheets to reveal his back.

Eric took one look and snorted.

'What's so funny?' Morgan peered over his shoulder.

'Strawberries. You look like a leper. I can't do this with that all over you.'

'Are you really going to stop now?'

'No, I've got a better idea.' Eric put his hands on Morgan's shoulders and pushed. As the other man flattened beneath him, Eric ran his hands along those thick, muscled arms and stretched them towards the top of the bed.

'Stay like that,' he murmured.

Pulling back became a tease, trailing his fingertips over Morgan's skin until he shuddered against the bed.

When certain that he wouldn't move, Eric licked at the juice and pulped strawberries.

Each flick of his tongue made the bigger man shift against the bed.

'I said, stay like that.'

'You're making it bloody difficult.'

'Try harder.' Nuzzling against the soft patch of skin above Morgan's hip, Eric lapped up another squashed strawberry before nipping the pink tinged

flesh beneath. 'I'm not fucking you until you're clean. The longer it takes . . .'
He teased one finger over the smooth skin of Morgan's backside. He
pushed between the cheeks and wriggled deeper, seeking out the tight
pucker of flesh that was his eventual destination.

'Get on with it.'

Though he knew his lover well, Eric never ceased to enjoy the effect
they had on each other. When he heard the tense breathlessness in
Morgan's voice, he felt an answering tingle course through his skin. Cords
of pleasure tightened on his gut and chest, squeezing until he felt short of
breath himself.

A single line of strawberries remained. Their smell perfumed the air with
such sweetness that for a short moment Eric imagined he might be
dreaming. He closed his eyes and inhaled, sucking in the scent of fruit,
burning wax and sex.

A stinging slap against his thigh jerked him back to the present.

'I swear, if you leave me hanging like this . . .!'

He looked down again.

Morgan's face shone beneath a thin film of sweat. His narrowed eyes
burned with impatience and passion. 'Well?'

'Put your head back down.'

Though he swore and rolled his eyes, Morgan did as instructed.

Once more Eric lowered his head. Starting at the nape, he ran his
tongue down Morgan's spine with one long stroke. He picked up
strawberry juice on the way, a lingering slick of cream and the salty tang of
sweat. Hovering over the double dimple at the base of his spine, he licked
again, all the way back up until Morgan began to moan into the pillows
bunched beneath his face.

Eric saw his fingers twitch, then grip the sheets.

'Ready?' he asked.

'Yes, yes, yes. Hurry up, before I burst.'

Kneeling between Morgan's thighs, Eric snatched a spare pillow and
tucked it beneath his hips. The resulting angle was pleasing enough to make
his cock jerk and his nipples harden. He teased the little pucker with his
thumb then pulled the latex glove over his hand. It took a lot of fumbling
to get the fingers in place but eventually his hand was sheathed to match his
eager cock.

Again he touched Morgan's hole, though this time with an ounce more
pressure.

'Christ on a bike, Eric,' Morgan groaned into his pillow. 'If you don't
stick your fingers in me right now I'll fucking punch you.'

'Okay, okay. Where did the lube go?'

'Fuck's sake!'

Eric scoured the bed until he found the tube. His slippery fingers fumbled the lid and a great arc of clear jelly shot into the air. It splattered the sheets in a long, damp line.

Laughter bubbled from his mouth. 'Sorry. Okay. I'm ready.' After gathering some of the spillage on to his fingers he used his free hand to spread Morgan's rear cheeks.

At last he saw his lover's unobstructed entrance, a tiny hole which he knew, with the right treatment, would open before him like a flower in bloom.

Slick, cool gel against hot, sticky flesh. The different sensations made him groan.

A little pressure and the tip of his finger popped through the little opening. He paused.

'You okay? You're all stiff.'

'It's been a while.' Morgan's breath caught as a ragged gasp. Then, slowly, his shoulders and back relaxed. Tension flowed from his legs and arse. He sighed. 'Okay, keep going.'

Eric obeyed, pushing until the first knuckle slipped in. Then the second.

The tight grip on his probing digit reminded him of a warm glove; old and well worn, used to the contours of his flesh. He twisted the finger round, then back again and once more saw Morgan clutch the pillows.

'Fuck, that's good. Keep going.'

The words sent an electric pulse through his body. The pleasurable tingles coursed down and pooled in his cock. His hips jerked forward and, for a moment, he doubted his ability to wait.

A deep breath. A kiss on the rounded curve of Morgan's arse. The musk of his arousal stung Eric's nose.

He steadied himself to add another finger.

'Ready?'

'God, yes. Do it.'

Eric ran his middle finger in alongside his index.

'Yes . . .' More pillow clutching.

As he watched the muscles tense and relax across his lover's shoulders, Eric waited for the silent signal to continue. When it came he added his ring finger, forced to exert more pressure to find passage.

With three fingers seated inside Morgan's body, Eric began to pull back. Slowly with a slight twist to spread the lube around. When he felt his boyfriend relax further around his hand, he began an easy pumping motion. His other hand reached around and gripped his straining cock.

Morgan mewled into the pillow, bucking his hips up and down, stepping up the tempo. 'Eric, please. Fuck me now.'

The desperation living in Morgan's voice proved to be Eric's undoing. He growled and eased his fingers free. They slid easily, gliding on a bed of lube.

He pulled on Morgan's hips. 'On your knees,' he said.

Instant compliance. Morgan even lowered his head and pushed his rear higher into the air, panting like a racing dog.

Eric steadied himself against Morgan's back, then guided his eager prick towards that waiting, winking hole. His entry resembled surfing on velvet, or gliding on ice. No pain, no resistance, just a faint grunt as his tip broke past the first ring of muscle. Then on and beyond, Morgan's body sucking him in greedily.

Inch by glorious inch, Eric watched his cock disappear inside Morgan's willing body. The muscles closed around his shaft, hugging him, squeezing him, threatening to send him spiralling off into pleasure overload.

Eric froze. Every part of his body coiled tight and he bit hard on his bottom lip. He closed his eyes. Thought of dirty socks. Vacuuming. Simone. Anything at all to fight off the orgasm approaching at a startling pace.

Morgan trembled beneath him. Beads of sweat slid down the back of his neck.

Eric licked one and savoured the explosion of salt on his tongue. 'Mmm,' he moaned.

'Christ, I forgot how good this feels.' Morgan released the breath he'd been holding and pushed up into a kneeling position, careful to keep himself fully impaled.

The changed angle forced Eric to tilt his hips and, as he did so, he splayed his hands across Morgan's chest. The other man leaned against him, craning his neck for a kiss that Eric gave immediately.

He slipped his tongue into Morgan's eager mouth and caught the flavour of strawberries coupled with his own unique taste.

Panting, Eric yanked off the glove and tossed it aside. He longed to feel Morgan's skin beneath his own. With bold strokes, he caressed his boyfriend's chest. The spirals of hair. The hard nubs of his nipples. More hair formed a line between those firm points and travelled down, a trail that spread out on to his stomach.

He teased them while rocking his hips, alternating between pulling, stroking, kneading and tickling. Each motion brought a fresh sound from Morgan's lips and made his cock dribble.

Eric made a game of trying to vary those sounds, occasionally increasing his pace or slowing to an agonising crawl of motion. Each time he slowed, Morgan thrust down with his backside, wriggling from side to side as if those impatient movements might encourage a faster pace.

Eric nipped him on the side of the neck. Then on the shoulder. He watched the pale marks slowly fill with flushed colour while Morgan cried words that made no sense. Then he did it again, over and over, across those sweaty arms, the shoulders, the neck, until sweat and Morgan's own delicious flavour consumed everything.

'Harder.'

Eric blinked. Paused around a mouthful of flesh. 'What?'

Morgan thrust back with his hips. 'Don't stop. I said harder!'

This time Eric didn't hesitate. He freed his teeth from Morgan's shoulder and gave him a shove. The other man dropped back on to his hands with a yelp, but Eric didn't waste time checking on him. Instead, he gripped those sweaty hips, spread his own knees and began a fresh rhythm of thrusting.

A moan bubbled through Morgan's lips, so long it seemed to have no end. He put his head down, braced his upper body against his crossed arms, and pushed back on to Eric.

The grip on his cock was exquisite; a combination of heat, pressure and delicious friction. His skin tingled all over. His head raced and the rasp of his laboured breathing joined Morgan's in ecstatic harmony.

'Fuck,' he whispered. 'Fuck.' His pace became sketchy, his vision misty.

'I'm close.' Morgan's whisper strained like a taut elastic band. He shuddered.

Eric freed one hand and grabbed his lover's cock instead, instantly appreciative of the hot dribble of pre-orgasmic release washing over his fingers.

'Harder. Faster. Fuck. Yes, Eric. Christ, yes.' Morgan's moans faded into an incoherent stream of expletives.

Eric gave one last jerk and felt his boyfriend explode. Hot bursts flooded over his hand, slicking up his fingers as he continued to thrust. Morgan wailed but he refused to let him go, pumping that trembling shaft until the cream stopped flowing.

When he was certain there was no more, Eric resumed thrusting, marvelling at the fact that Morgan's cock was still rock hard.

The idea that their pleasure might continue made him pump even harder. One thrust, two, three, as if he sought to burst through and come out the other side.

'Go on, Eric,' Morgan hissed. 'Let me feel you come. I want to feel you let go.'

Extra pressure, combined with the filthy talk propelled Eric towards exactly that. He held on for as long as he could, gritting his teeth, holding it in, but then Morgan's groping hands reached beneath them and brushed his balls. That last piece of stimulation shattered the remaining vestige of control.

Eric closed his eyes, tipped his head back, and managed one last thrust before giving in. A moan clawed from his throat, long and deep while tiny spasms coursed through his legs and arms. Stars of white and purple exploded across the inside of his eyelids and the coiling sensation in his gut sprang loose, firing darts of ecstasy along every nerve.

It went on for hours, days . . . He couldn't tell, lost in the bright, skin-tingling well of pleasure.

He slumped across Morgan's back and lay there gasping. 'Holy hell.'

'You okay?'

'Fine,' he whispered, 'just give me a second.'

Morgan snorted. 'Don't mind me.'

When Eric next opened his eyes he saw Morgan staring at him from over his shoulder. He exhaled and watched his breath rustle Morgan's curly hair.

'Fuck me . . .'

'Maybe later.' Morgan grinned. 'For now I need to move.'

'What?' The room had fuzzy edges. Dancing candlelight and flickering shadow made Eric sleepy.

'Cramp. I need to move.'

'Oh, come on.'

'No, seriously. Get off.' Morgan crawled forward.

Eric yelped. The glove of Morgan's arse slid down his cock with a sensation that made him long for another try. 'No, no, wait a second. Please, I can't—'

'I can't feel my legs.'

After a few seconds of fumbling, tilting and grunting, Eric managed to ease them both on to the mattress on their sides. Within Morgan's body, Eric's cock finally began to soften which he took as a sign to ease himself free. He bit his lip as the sensations sent another rush of pleasure shooting up and down his legs.

Morgan rolled to face him. 'Sorry, but cramp. You okay?'

'I should be asking you that. Was it too much?'

He grinned. 'Hell no. If I knew you had that in you I'd have suggested it months ago.'

Eric chuckled and eased the condom off his wilting member. He tied a knot in the end. 'I learned from the best.'

'Cheesy, dude. Fucking cheesy.'

He yawned. 'Whatever. Can we sleep now?'

Morgan looked pointedly at the squashed strawberries and spilt cream.

'Oh, come on!' Eric sighed.

'If you want to sleep in a strawberry-spunk compote be my guest. I'll take the spare room.' He clambered into a kneeling position and prepared to hop off the bed.

'No way, this was your idea.' Lunging, Eric grabbed Morgan around the waist. The pair of them, carried by his momentum, sailed off the bed and on to the floor and the rest of the strawberries. The sticky duvet slithered down on top of them.

Eric pulled it off his head and wiped a slick of red juice from his cheek. 'New house rule; no food in bed.' Standing, he wrapped the duvet into a ball and tossed it against the wall. 'Agreed?'

'What about no food in our bed? What's the point in having a spare room if we don't take advantage of it every now and then?'

'Indeed. Though next time you try to seduce me can you do it in the bathroom or something? Or use less messy food?'

Morgan's eyes sparkled in the candle light. 'But what about the melting chocolate I've got downstairs?'

The thought almost broke through Eric's veneer of fatigue. 'Next time, so long as you let me lick every damn ounce of it off your skin. Deal?'

'Deal.'

SIMONE & MR BRADFORD

Simone tilted her head back and stifled a moan with the back of her hand. The sound of approaching footsteps brought her gaze up, but she didn't stop moving. She flexed her fingers. Sighed. Bucked her hips. Her thumb pushed past the barrier of her knickers and rubbed. *Oh god, just a bit more. Ten seconds . . .*

A disembodied voice floated through the closed door. 'I just need another pack of staples.'

Shafts of pale gold light speared into the tiny cupboard as the door opened.

Simone dropped her hand from beneath her skirt, and whirled to face the tall shelves stacked with stationary supplies. Sweat beaded on her forehead and dripped into her eyes. Her heart raced. Tingles of pleasure shot up and down her legs. She fought it and wobbled towards a row of notebooks, yanking two from the stack.

'Oh, hey. Didn't know there was anyone in here.'

Simone turned. Glared. Morgan Fenton stared back, his narrow green tie snugged tight against his neck. He frowned, gaze skimming over her face before pausing on the notebooks clutched in her trembling hand. 'Didn't you just get some of those? There's about six on our workstation.'

'Oh.' She shoved them back into place. 'You're right. Sorry.'

He stroked his jaw. 'You okay? You look flustered.'

'I'm fine. I need pens.'

'Over there.' Morgan hooked a thumb over his shoulder.

'Thanks.' Slinking past him, aware of his gaze on her back, Simone approached the shelves. Boxes of pens, highlighters and pencils lined the highest shelf. She paused to wipe sweat from her forehead.

So close. She selected three black and two blue biros. *Three seconds, that's all I needed. Five tops.*

Soft rustling sounds accompanied Morgan's own search for supplies. He cursed, then kicked a box of printer paper. 'Have you seen the staples?'

Simone barely knew where she was let alone anything else. Frustration boiled through her. 'No, I bloody haven't.'

'Wow, sorry I asked. Are you done in here?'

She squeezed past him towards the door. 'Yes, why?'

'Your skirt is tucked into your pants. Thought you'd like to know before going back to your desk.'

Simone slapped her hands to her hips, sliding down the line of her grey pencil skirt. Sure enough, as her fingers reached mid-thigh she found the fabric looped under, tucked up towards her waist. Beneath it, her thighs gleamed with slick, musky moisture.

'Shit!' She yanked it back into place, avoiding his gaze. More expletives streamed from her mouth.

Morgan howled with laughter and gripped the edge of a nearby cabinet.

'You waited this long to tell me? What's wrong with you? Freaking pervert!'

'Says the woman frigging in the stationary cupboard.'

Simone winced. His continued laughter made her fingers itch. She longed to punch him. Instead she folded her arms to hide her nipples, still erect and sensitive. 'Fuck you.'

'No thanks. And don't worry, I won't tell anyone.'

Panic replaced fury. 'No one would believe you anyway.'

'You think? I reckon most folks would take pity on you after such a dry weekend.'

'Meaning?' She grabbed a tube of computer screen wipes and snagged one to wipe her thighs.

'I heard you got shot down at Vicki's party. Spent all night chasing a gay guy.'

Simone froze. 'Who told you that?'

'Just . . . someone.'

'Well it's not true. And it's none of your damn business.'

'Touchy. Didn't it go well?'

She thought back, wading through the drunken fog to find a memory that made sense.

Flashes of faces. Snatches of conversation. A bathroom. A man sitting in the bathtub with a look of disgust and horror on his face.

'It went fine,' she lied. 'I had a great time.'

'Good for you.' Morgan finally found his staples and opened the door. 'Don't be too long. *Madford* is on the warpath; something about a client bill putting us over quota.'

Dragging her mind back to work matters took Simone longer than it should have. She sucked her teeth. 'We're all in the shit then.'

'Yep.' Morgan walked out, leaving the door ajar.

Alone again, Simone released a weary breath. She pressed both hands to her face. The smell of sex filled her nose, firing her senses with longing. She sucked each finger then cleaned them with another screen wipe.

After one last check of her skirt and legs she left the cupboard.

At her desk, Simone slumped into her chair and lowered her head to the keyboard. Her computer shrieked in complaint, opened a blank file and filled it with a line of 'G's.

Rae looked up from beyond the narrow desk divide. 'What's wrong?' She cracked chewing gum between her nicotine stained teeth. 'Lost your data sheets again?'

Simone lifted her head. The computer stopped typing 'G'. 'I'm fine.'

'Lies,' said Rae, cheerfully. 'You look like someone gave you a fanny wedgie. How was the party?'

'Fine,' roared Simone, ignoring startled gasps from a desk nearby. 'I tried to pull and it blew up in my face. The guy was gay, okay? I didn't know and he blew me off in the bathroom. Happy now?'

A soft snicker came from direction of the coffee machine. Morgan smirked at her over the rim of his mug. He waved and sauntered back to his desk, still tittering.

Rae cocked her head. 'I was only asking. What gay guy?'

A little of Simone's rage leaked away. Embarrassment flushed her cheeks with warmth. 'You didn't know?'

'How would I? You've barely said a word all morning and most of that time you've been in the bloody stationary cupboard.'

'How come Morgan knows if you don't?'

'No idea. Ask him.'

The thought of going anywhere near that smirking cretin made Simone's stomach writhe. She settled for glaring at him over the top of her computer before returning her attention to Rae. She lowered her voice. 'Remember Bill?'

'The cute one?'

'If you say so. Vicki's brother. He spent the whole night trying to get in my knickers.'

Rae cracked her gum again. 'Great. He's a stud.'

'He's a dick. And I blew him off for Eric.'

'I don't know him.'

'Me neither. But he's super-cute, built like a Greek statue, eyes like diamonds. So of course he's gay.'

A wince from Rae. 'Sorry hon, that sucks.'

'Why are the cute ones always gay?'

'Bill isn't.'

Simone glared at her computer screen, drumming her fingers on the desk. 'Bill's still pining over Hiral. I don't want her left-overs.'

'So you went for the gay guy instead?' Rae arched an eyebrow.

Another whine came from the computer as Simone slapped the keyboard with her fist. 'It's not fair. I just want a shag.' Her denied sex gave another tingle as she remembered how close to release she'd been in the stationary cupboard.

Just another few seconds. Damn you, Morgan.

On the other side of the office, the main lift pinged. When the doors opened, a sack of money on legs stalked through. Or that's how it felt to Simone. Amos 'Madford' Bradford probably spent more on a single suit than Simone did on her monthly rent, and it showed in every perfect crease and seam.

'Shit,' Simone scrabbled to make sense of the clutter on her desk. 'Arsehole alert.'

Rae ducked behind the divide. The clack of furious typing soon replaced the sound of her voice.

As Simone deleted the page of 'G's and opened an existing letter, a shadow fell over her desk. 'Miss Daye, do you have the next batch of letters to countersign?'

Not even a 'good morning'? We're totally screwed if he's already in a shitty mood.

She looked up. Bit her lip. 'Yes sir.' Despite herself, Simone couldn't help but look him over with a grudging sense of appreciation.

Bradford boasted brown hair, full and shiny though streaked with grey. But for faint lines around the eyes, his skin was unwrinkled. Behind the frames of his designer glasses sharp, lively eyes assessed and judged her.

'Bring them to my office. My afternoon meeting got pulled forward so I won't be able to do it later.'

'Yes, Sir. Coming.'

He marched away, though the double doors leading to the far side of the building.

While scrabbling through the bombsite of her desk, Simone heard Morgan tittering again. She straightened. 'What's funny?'

'Nothing.' He pulled on his coat. 'I'm going to lunch.'

'You're not until slot three.'

'I swapped with Rae. I have a date.'

Rae flushed and ducked her head.

'Thanks. So I'm managing Bradford and the phones alone today?' Simone crunched a sheet of paper beneath her fingers.

'Aah, you can handle it. Just use your sexy, feminine whiles.' More smirking.

The lift doors pinged again. Opened. When she saw who stood in the opening, Simone's stomach plummeted into her toes.

'Shit!' She ducked behind her desk. Scrunched her eyes shut.

Embarrassment boiled through her insides.

Rae's face appeared over the divide. 'What are you doing?'

'Is he still there?'

'Who?'

'Eric. He just came out the lift.'

'The post guy?'

Simone's guts knotted. 'He works here?'

'He's from the delivery unit.' Rae's eyes widened. She gave a little shriek. 'No-fucking-way.'

Against every scrap of common sense, Simone gave in to her curiosity and stood.

Near the lift stood Eric. Just like at the party, his strong body and soulful eyes caught Simone's attention and held it. Without the fog of alcohol she could remember how good his breath had smelled while everyone else stank of lager and pizza.

Beside him, one arm draped across his slender shoulders stood Morgan. She gripped her blouse. 'Fuck.'

Morgan wrapped both arms around Eric's shoulders and kissed him on the lips. Eric responded eagerly, even going so far as to stroke his cheek.

Rae spat her gum at the bin. 'Damn. I had my suspicions, but I never thought I'd see it. Morgan Fenton: big fairy.'

Simone watched the pair leave. The heat in her face intensified as Eric caught her eye just before the lift doors closed. His lips tightened as he recognised her. Then Morgan grinned and gave a snarky wave. The doors slid shut.

At least I know how he found out. She returned to gathering letters. *Shit, why did it have to be him? I don't care that he's gay, but why did he have to be with Morgan Fenton? Fuck, fuck, fuck.*

Her grip crumpled the printed pages as she carried them across the office. Her shoulders prickled and each low whisper or sidelong glance seemed to prove her worst fears.

The whole office knew. Morgan told everyone and now they were laughing at her.

Shame mingled with anger as she shoved the double doors open and entered the adjoining corridor.

Tears filled her eyes. Her steps became heavy and stiff.

It's not fair.

Tears trickled down her face and onto the letters.

Get a grip. You can't let Madford see you like this.

Just thinking of her boss drove the tears away. She took a deep breath in then out, repeated four times until the tears dried up.

Three more seconds to wipe her face, straighten her hair, then Simone stepped from the world of the worker-ant into that of the corporate elite.

Everything, from the carpets to the desks themselves, was large and expensive. She passed the coffee machine, noting that these machines vended their goodies without the need of a prepay keycard.

Instead of cardboard, faux leather divides in shades of brown and royal blue separated each desk. The large windows overlooked the park rather than a brick wall. Framed awards and certificates dotted the walls.

Sectioned off from the main floor plan, three private offices lined the rear wall.

She tapped on the door farthest to the left.

A muffled, 'One moment,' came from inside.

Simone adjusted her grip on the papers. Tapped her foot. Sighed. Straightened her skirt.

Eventually she turned and gazed back into the main office. It was quiet but for the clack of fingers on keyboards and the one-sided murmur of telephone conversations. Some faces glanced her way but people on this side of the huge office mostly kept to themselves.

They even dress different.

A blonde woman in three inch heels and loose grey trousers strode to her desk. As if sensing her audience, the woman shot Simone a stern stare before picking up her phone.

Simone faced the door, resisting the urge to knock a second time.

Her gaze flicked up to the fancy lettering on the shiny gold name plate.

AMOS BRADFORD ESQ

MANAGING DIRECTOR

Now there was a man worth worrying over. Mature. Rich. Sexy, even with, or *because* of, his foul moods and worse language.

She nibbled her bottom lip.

Everybody knew that Bradford hated his gold-digging wife. They understood that his relationship at home bled into his working life, forcing everyone to walk on eggshells until sure of his mood. The worst kept secret in the world was that Mrs Bradford refused to sign divorce papers. Clearly she saw more profit in maintaining her marriage to the businessman who alternated his Jaguar with his Ferrari three days a week.

'Come in.' His voice splintered Simone's thoughts.

After a brief hesitation she opened the door.

Bradford stood by his desk with his back to her, the expensive fabric of his jacket drawn tight over his squash-player's shoulders. A curl of dark hair tumbled over his collar. When he turned, his shirt buttons strained over a chest tight with muscle.

She looked at his face, but his gaze aimed lower, straight at a gap in her blouse.

Morgan, that arse! He couldn't tell me I'd lost a button?

She cleared her throat and tried not to think about how much of her bra was on display. 'Sir, I have the letters for countersigning.'

He looked up, at last, and instead of meeting her gaze, glanced at his computer screen. 'Bring them here.'

Why did that brusque order sound like so much more?

As she walked, Simone's heels sank into the lush carpet. Burgundy and tasteful, just like everything else, from the oak table – twice the size of hers – to the leather chair behind it.

She stood near his desk, waiting for an invitation to sit. It never came.

'How many today?' He didn't look away from the screen.

It took Simone several seconds to figure out what he meant. 'Twelve,' she blurted. 'There'll be more this afternoon, but some of the calculations need double checking.'

Bradford blew a heavy breath through his nose. His gaze dropped back to her breasts then flicked up again, lightening quick. 'How much in total?'

She squirmed. '£16,000.'

Silence.

'I said—'

'I heard what you said, Miss Daye. I'm just surprised. I thought we were doing well this month.'

Simone licked her lips. Not for the first time she inwardly cursed Rae and her happy trigger finger when agreeing compensation. 'Many customers had good cases, Sir. Their complaints are the result of major staff errors.'

A snort. 'Make sure it's in the monthly report. I want to know who's lost their bonus this year.'

'Yes, Sir.'

That said, Bradford snagged the stack of papers from her grip and skim-read them. He scrawled his signature at the bottom of each. His lips twitched as he read, the icy blue of his eyes dancing back and forth as he skimmed the text. Twice he snorted, once he outright growled and slashed his signature across the page with a ferocity that almost tore the paper.

At the last letter, he paused.

Simone held her breath. It was one of hers.

'£3,000?' He glanced up. 'To one person?'

'Yes. The customer lost four days of business due to a faulty machine. She also had a break-in—'

'Not our problem.' Bradford narrowed his eyes.

She squirmed. 'No . . . but the FSA is involved. I've already talked her down from £20,000—'

'Excuse me?'

Gazing into his eyes, Simone knew she had no need to repeat herself. This time she waited, watching his face for clues of his mood.

'£20,000? And you talked her down?'

'I was talking to her for an hour, but I did it.'

Amos Bradford smiled. The change to his face was alarming.

Wrinkles vanished from around his eyes and a small dimple puckered his left cheek. Frown lines smoothed out and the darkness filling his gaze melted away. He looked almost young.

'Impressive. Very impressive.'

'Thanks.' She risked a smile.

Bradford signed the last page with an extravagant flourish. His pen flew from his fingers, hit the desk and bounced to the floor. 'Grab that, will you?'

What am I, your maid?

Simone ducked and groped for it. The pen slid away and rolled beneath the desk. 'Damn.'

'Problem?'

She cringed, biting her lip over the answer she longed to give. 'No, I'll get it.' She wedged herself beneath the table. Her fingers brushed something soft, lain over something hard and long. Confused she gripped tighter. It flexed.

Fuck, that's his calf. He's ripped like an Olympic runner!

Before she could pull her hand back, Simone heard a knock at the office door.

'Come in,' said Bradford at once. His leg flexed beneath her hand again, then slid forward to stroke her arm.

What the hell? She pulled away. He followed, nudging her fingers with his toe.

'Sir—'

The office door opened.

Simone squeaked, conscious of her rear sticking up from beneath the desk.

'Hi, Amos,' a chirpy female voice filled the room. 'Your wife is on line six.'

What the hell must I look like? Maybe the chair hides me. Jesus, was he really playing footsie with me?

Hardly daring to breathe, Simone waited.

Bradford grunted. 'Tell her I'll call back. I'm not done with Simone.'

She cringed at the mention of her name. No hiding now.

'Who?' The female voice came closer.

Simone abandoned the pen and crawled out from beneath the table. She did it fast, eager to be on her feet instead of her knees.

The woman in the doorway lifted her eyebrows. 'Oh.'

Shit, it's the blonde one.

'Tell Dianne I'll call her back later.' Bradford bent to retrieve his pen. He seemed not to notice the tension in the room as he beckoned Simone closer.

She hurried around the desk, as if placing a physical object between herself and the other woman might prevent further embarrassment.

The moment she stood still, a firm hand grasped the back of her knee and slid up beneath her skirt.

Simone froze. She glanced down but Bradford's eyes were focused on his secretary, his smile steady and innocent.

He's touching me. Fuck, he's totally copping a feel.

'Anything else, Mel? I'm busy.'

His hand teased higher, one finger tracing lazy spirals on the back of her thigh. Higher.

Fuck. Fuck, fuck, fuck!

'No, I've got it. Thanks, Amos.' Mel gave him a lingering look before leaving. The door clicked shut.

Simone remained frozen. Her skin tingled beneath Bradford's confident, roaming hand which now switched back and forth between her trembling thighs.

'Sir . . .?'

'Yes?'

'Your hand—'

He cut her off by squeezing the flesh beneath the line of her damp knickers. 'You did great work with that customer, Miss Daye. *Simone.*' His fingernails scraped her sensitive skin.

She shuddered and locked her knees. 'Thanks.'

'Our figures would be even worse if we had to fork out £20,000 on top of the other issues. You've saved us a lot of money.'

'Just doing my job.' Her words rasped over a tongue as dry as paper. She licked her lips. It didn't help. Her mind, her attention, everything focused on the teasing tickle of his finger. Warm. Smooth. Firm. Most of all, confident, as if she were a car or golf club he considered buying.

'Good.' His fingers touched her knickers and stopped. He stroked the gusset then pressed inward. Her damp slit parted easily to let his finger through, grinding the fabric against her most delicate areas.

Sweet Jesus that feels good.

As if sensing her thoughts he smiled. 'What happened here?'

She couldn't think straight. His finger worked a familiar, dangerous magic, switching between soft and firm pressure.

'I spilt some coffee.'

'No you didn't.' Just like every other time he spoke, Bradford's voice resonated with calm confidence. Only this time amusement was there too.

A finger burrowed beneath the elastic of one leg hole. He sucked in a sharp breath. 'How long have you worked here?'

Are you serious? I don't know!

'Simone?' His finger stopped moving.

71

'Um . . . three years, or something. I'm not sure.'

'Three years. And you still write letters for Complaints?' As he spoke, Bradford resumed exploring with his finger. The tip brushed the curls of hair at the base of her slit before curving up.

So soon after her aborted attempt in the stationary cupboard, this calm, confident touch rekindled her lust almost instantly. A spiral of pleasure filled her belly and began to spin its way outward.

'I applied for a role on the corporate side, but I didn't get it. Not experienced enough.'

A chuckle. 'You seem pretty *experienced* to me.' Without moving his finger, Bradford leaned across to his phone. He dialled with his other hand. 'Mel, bring me the list of recent vacancies. I want to check something.' A pause. 'No, bring it now.' He hung up.

A bolt of horror shot through Simone's body. She tried to step sideways but Bradford snaked out his free hand and grabbed her hip. He held her in place with an arm around her waist, all without pausing the motions of his intruding finger.

The thought of being seen this way made Simone groan. Her nipples stiffened beneath her clothing. A rush of confusion consumed her and she squeezed her eyes shut. 'What are you doing?'

Bradford grinned, exposing his perfect teeth. 'Checking the vacancy list. There's one in Accounts perfect for a woman of your *skills*.' His finger sank into her moist slit as far as the second knuckle.

Gasping, Simone pushed on tiptoes. His hand followed, rising until her skirt bunched on his wrist. She gripped the edge of the desk until her knuckles whitened. 'Fuck . . . oh god.'

She wanted to scream. To dismount his finger and run from the room shrieking as loud as she could. But one part of her resisted. A large, frustrated part of her longed to rock back and forth on his hand until he completed what she started such a short time ago. The conflict made her head ache.

'You're soaking wet, did you realise?' He stood just far enough to whisper into her ear. 'Your cunt is leaking all over my shirt sleeves.'

Her eyes flashed open. She never imagined he could talk in such a way, nor that she would like it so much.

Surprise at his language came second to shock as a bolt of pleasure shot through her body.

He curled his finger, crooking it forward until the tip scraped the little bundle of nerves that made her want to shout and laugh and scream.

The office door swung open.

Mel marched in holding a stack of papers.

Simone didn't dare look at her.

Surely she knew what was going on. She could see. Surely this stuffy blonde could smell the musk of her over-excited slit, screaming for mercy.

Mel flicked her hair and set the papers on the table. 'Anything else, Amos?'

Calm and cool as ever, Bradford shook his head. 'No.'

Another finger grazed Simone's pussy before sliding in, joining the first to perform a gentle but highly effective stretching motion.

Mel nodded, then left.

The door barely clicked shut before Simone let loose her cry. She shuddered beneath his expert touch.

Galvanised at last, she clutched his hand. 'Are you crazy?'

'I'll stop if you want.' He sounded disappointed.

'No.' Simone spoke without thinking. When she heard the desperation in her voice, her stomach ached with shame. But her pussy pulsed with an urgent need and rejoiced in the promise of salvation.

Bradford laughed. It was a full, rich sound. Smooth and sweet like lashings of melted chocolate laced with caramel. 'I thought not. It must be nice having someone else do the work.'

The rising pleasure hit a snag. 'Excuse me?'

'You think I don't know everything that goes on around here? Everything?'

The sudden flush of heat to her face had nothing to do with the magical motions of his invading fingers. Over her shoulder, she could see the older man's smile and quirk of his eyebrows.

'Fuck . . .'

'Not yet. But I can fix that for you if you'd like.'

The sensations spun a wicked spell around her, tempered only a little by embarrassment. It was exciting. She squeezed her thighs around his hand. He gave a moan of appreciation. She made one last attempt to save face.

'I don't know what you mean.'

'You do. For reasons I don't understand our stationary cupboard has become the favoured meeting place for horny staff members.' He finally pulled his intruding fingers away and yanked her down on to his lap. 'Maybe I'm working you too hard.'

'I like hard things.' The words left her mouth before she could think, but Simone couldn't help it. He was hard, an insistent presence against her rear as she rocked back and forth over him. His obvious desire for her banished her previous reservations and reminded her that she could be wanted, Eric and his gay preferences be damned.

She looked back over her shoulder. Bradford stared at her, his gaze hot and intense. He trailed a damp, musky finger over her lip, moaning when she sucked it in.

'Go lock the door,' he whispered.

With her skirt still bunched around her waist, Simone broke free and obeyed. When she turned back, Bradford already had his jacket and tie off. He unfastened his shirt buttons while staring at her, humming under his breath.

'Stop.' Simone frowned. 'Leave it on.'

He hesitated.

'How much time do you think we have? I get enough shit from Morgan about my personal life, I'd rather not give him ammunition.'

'Morgan Fenton?'

'Yep.'

Bradford nodded. 'Sharp lad. Observant. Wasted in complaints.'

'He's an arsehole.'

'Take off your pants, Simone.'

She froze near the door. 'What?'

'Take. Off. Your pants.' His voice changed. No longer soft and cajoling, but hard and commanding. The voice of the managing director. Sexy as hell.

Though her pussy throbbed and longed for further contact, her imagination ran wild picturing conduct reviews and the eventual thud of a P45 on her doorstep.

But the weekend of disappointment and the interruption in the cupboard conspired to rob her senses. Nothing mattered more than satisfying the ache between her thighs. If this sexy, grumpy man was willing, how could she turn him down?

She tucked her fingers into the waistband of her soaked knickers and drew them down. They hit the floor around her ankles.

'Wait.' Bradford leaned forward, licking his lips.

'What?'

'You look amazing.'

'I look like a slut.' She snapped, fighting to hide the breathless excitement she felt.

Bradford said nothing.

Simone stepped free of the undergarment, scooped it up and hurled it at Bradford's face.

He caught it with graceful ease and pressed the damp lace against his mouth. His tongue flicked out. Licked. Then he pushed a small portion into his mouth and sucked. 'You taste delicious.'

A thrilling mix of excitement and terror shivered through Simone's body. She gazed at his perfect suit and greying hair. So different from Eric or even Bill and not just in looks. His easy confidence and commanding nature inspired a sense of safety and security as well as filthy decadence. This man knew what he wanted and how he intended to get it, an attitude as thrilling as it was intimidating.

Simone lingered near the door, gazing at her feet.

'Come here.' He whispered.

She went to him, aware of the juices running down her thigh, the slipperiness of her skin beneath the deluge from her pussy. When she stopped before him, he tucked her skirt hem into her waistband.

Never before had she felt so exposed. So dirty.

So ready for a fucking shag!

Bradford trailed his hands along her thighs. He teased her navel, her stomach, then gripped her breasts and squeezed before cupping her cheeks.

Trapped, Simone had no choice but to accept the kiss. His tongue dived into her mouth, lashing against her gums and teeth. He tasted of expensive coffee and over that bitterness, she tasted her own pleasure, lingering on his lips like a clear balm.

The combination brought a moan from her lips.

He lifted her and dumped her on his desk, sweeping away pens and papers with brisk swipes of his hand. One hand on each thigh, he then shoved her legs apart and pushed his face towards her throbbing, tingling slit.

'You're so wet. Amazing.'

Bradford settled himself more securely on the floor and lashed out with his tongue, quick, darting motions all aimed at her throbbing clit. Within seconds Simone's fears were distant memory. She writhed across the desk.

He pushed a finger back inside her, then another, twisting both until they were covered with slick, clear juices. Like a trophy, he held up them up and eased them, one by one, into his mouth.

Fuck, where have you been all my life?

Simone gave another cry as he worked her pussy, alternating between licking, sucking and nibbling. He toyed with her, pushing her body further and further up the slope towards final release.

She closed her eyes, giving herself over to the wet sound of his tongue, the squelch of his fingers as he tucked them back inside. So much better than her own attempts. Harder. Faster.

His long digits pumped in and out of her body, twisting forward until the tips brushed against her g-spot. Her hips rocked forward off the table.

'Fuck, do me, already!' Pride no longer mattered. Nor did getting caught. Nothing mattered but the building orgasm threatening to shatter her into tiny pieces. 'What are you waiting for?'

'Stand up, turn over and lean over the desk.' Bradford tapped her arse as she obeyed. 'If fast is what you want, let's do that. You think it's just you gagging for a fuck?'

Simone heard something tear. She glanced over her shoulder just in time to see him roll a condom over the end of his cock. His trousers hung around his knees.

Where the hell was he keeping that? He's huge!

Her thoughts cut short as he gripped her hips. She squealed and grabbed the edge of the desk. His rough fingers bit into her skin as he dragged her into position. Paused. His tip grazed her rear cheeks before sliding between her thighs and arcing up into her warm depths. He slid inside with ease, his stiffness filling her utterly.

Christ, yes, this is what I need.

His entire girth rested inside her, long, thick and heavy. While gnawing her bottom lip Simone drew deep breaths through her nose. Her body relaxed around him. The sensation of fullness gave way to the tingle of mounting pleasure.

Bradford began a slow rocking motion, sliding out to his tip before driving back in.

She mewled against the table surface.

'Just what I need after a stressful morning.' He leaned over her back to nibble her earlobe. 'You're so wet. So fucking tight. Been a while?'

'None of your business.'

'Don't worry, Simone, tight pussy suits me.'

Simone longed to feel a rush of outrage but the building ecstasy wouldn't let her. After a long, unwilling drought, this was hard, fast and perfect.

Pressing her cheek to the desk, she spread her legs and braced herself.

Bradford must have felt the change because his grip tightened. The pace increased. He drove himself forward with rhythmic grunts loud enough to partially mask the slap of flesh against flesh.

'Yes.' His hot breath tickled her ear. 'That's right. You just lie there . . . lie there like a good little girl and let me fuck you the way you need it.'

Simone looked over her shoulder and found Bradford staring at the ceiling, his head tilted back until his Adam's apple strained against his throat. Then he leaned forward and grabbed her breasts through her blouse, squeezing hard.

She clenched her teeth and whined as her orgasm rushed to its peak.

I'm gonna come stretched over his desk. Flat on my stomach with my arse in the air like some kind of slut. Fuck, that's hot.

Simone and reached down to flick her swollen clit.

The gorged nub of flesh answered by firing shots of ecstasy through her body. Her toes curled. Sweat trickled down her forehead and down her jaw to drip off the end of her chin. Weakness crawled through her knees until her single coherent thought was relief that Bradford pressed her so firmly into the desk.

He slapped her arse, cracking the flat of his hand against her right cheek.

Despite her clenched teeth, a shriek burst from Simone's mouth. She thrashed across the desk, trapped beneath Bradford's weight. Her feet scrabbled against the floor then skidded out from under her until she lay flat and helpless beneath him. An instant later her orgasm broke and the force of it flattened senses with all the weight of an 18-wheeler.

The office faded away, the expensive desk, the carpet, the dozens of office workers less than thirty feet away.

Simone saw none of it, thought of none of it, just the detonation of pleasure stored and denied for three long months.

Pressed against her back, heavy and sweaty, Bradford stiffened, then moaned one long note. He gave three savage thrusts, tensed, then clamped his teeth on her shoulder through the blouse.

She gasped, choking down a scream as she bucked against him.

Long moments passed. The ecstasy ebbed. Sound and colour returned and Simone slowly came back to earth.

She released her over-sensitive clitoris and sighed into the table top. 'Wow.'

Bradford loosened his teeth from her shoulder and pulled away.

By the time Simone managed to stand straight, his softened cock had retreated back inside his trousers.

He cleared his throat and retrieved his tie. 'Leave the rest of the letters, Simone.' He glanced at the papers scattered across the floor. 'I'll bring them back before the close of business.'

The abrupt return to normal wiped the languid smile from Simone's lips. She rushed to adjust her blouse and tug her skirt down to its proper height. 'Um, sure. That's fine.'

'Good.' He pulled his suit jacket on then stooped to retrieve the detritus from his desk. 'I'll see you this afternoon.'

She stared at him open-mouthed. Little waves of pleasure continued to pulse through her body. The creamy moisture of her satisfied slit trickled down her trembling thighs. 'That's it?'

He glanced at her. 'Excuse me?'

'"See you this afternoon"? Is that all you've got?'

'What more do you want?'

A sour taste filled her mouth. A weight dropped into her stomach. 'But I thought—' She pursed her lips. 'Don't worry about it. Just give me back my knickers and I'll get out of here.' Rage swelled and overruled her confusion. She held out her hand. 'Well?'

Bradford stared. Without breaking eye contact he bent and retrieved the lacy garment from the ground. 'What knickers?' Chuckling, he opened a drawer in his desk, tucked them inside and slammed it shut.

Cold fingers of horror replaced the aftershocks of pleasure.

She lowered her voice, wary of her bunched fists and unsteady breathing. 'I've still got four hours to go. I can't fucking do that without pants.'

'Of course you can.' He pressed a button on the phone at the end of his desk. 'Mel?'

'Yes, Amos?' That familiar female voice issued from the speakers.

Simone slapped a hand over her mouth.

'Bring in the next batch of marketing reports. I want to read them before my meeting.' He released the button. 'Are you still here, Simone?'

She stared at him, words dying on the tip of her tongue. His steady gaze bored into hers until her stomach gave a flutter of fear. She looked at the floor, the desk, the awards lining the walls.

'I . . .' The giddy pleasure of moments ago vanished. A raw ache filled her chest. Her eyelids tingled. 'No, I'm going.'

Simone ran for the door. She unlocked it and flung it open, startled to find Mel already standing there, a blue folder in her hands.

'Excuse me,' Simone shoved by and marched towards the double doors. The whole time she kept her head high, her eyes forward, unwilling to see what jokes were being made as she left. As she reached the doors to the adjoining corridor, she caught a glimpse of Bradford's reflection in the glass. Still watching her. Smiling.

A sob bubbled from her lips. She fled.

Back at her desk, Simone squirmed and twisted on the chair, trying to find a position that didn't remind her of her lack of underwear. Traces of her juices slicked her thighs. Crossing her legs only made it worse.

The lift doors pinged, admitting Morgan and, if that weren't bad enough, Eric.

She cringed when they spotted her, begging the floor beneath her feet to open up and suck her in.

It didn't, of course.

She sniffed, wiped her eyes and waited.

'Hey, Simone.' Morgan raised a hand in a pitiful sort of half-wave.

'Not now,' she glared at her computer screen. 'This isn't a good time. Just leave me alone.'

'I'm not here to tease you.'

Something in his voice made her look up.

Morgan stood at the edge of her workstation, hands folded at waist height. Eyes downcast, he shifted from foot to foot and sighed as Eric gave him a rough jab in the back. 'I'm here to say sorry.'

Simone gaped.

'When I told Eric what happened this morning he made me promise to come in here and apologise, so here I am. Sorry I teased you. Sorry I made you feel like an idiot . . . even if you were one.'

Eric punched him in the arm.

'What? You told her you're gay and she wouldn't leave you alone. That is dumb.'

Eric cut in with a grim smile. 'What my idiot boyfriend means to say, is that he didn't mean to make an awkward situation any worse. You didn't do any harm, we've all come out of it unharmed and unmolested. Mostly. I'm sorry too. I could have handled it better.'

Staring into Eric's big blue eyes, Simone couldn't help but wonder about his choices. Not that she knew much about him, but the pair didn't seem to *fit*. Him short and broad, Morgan, tall and gangling, they resembled mismatched dolls more than any couple she knew. He was just too . . . nice.

Unlike some arseholes I know.

'I didn't exactly make it easy.' She fought the urge to offer her own apologies. Instead she settled for: 'I was pretty drunk.'

Eric smiled. 'More than you realise, but the apology stands. I hope we can put it behind us.'

'Sure. Whatever.'

'Great. I need to get back to work.' Eric kissed Morgan's cheek. 'See you later.' He walked away.

Morgan watched him go then sighed and slouched back to his desk. 'I really am sorry. I didn't think you'd cry about it.'

She flinched. 'I didn't cry.' Even as she said it, heat filled her cheeks.

'Really? Because your face is all red and blotchy. Your hair's a mess and I'm sure your skirt is back to front. Or is that from before?'

That last reminder of her terrible mistake was more than she could stand. Simone surged to her feet. 'Fuck you, Morgan. Just . . . fuck you.'

Ignoring his startled cry, she fled the desk, back into the adjoining corridor and the stationary cupboard.

She leaned against the door. Tears streamed down her cheeks.

Idiot. Idiot, idiot! How could I? How could I do that? With my boss?

'. . . so hot. I think she's the one, babe.' The familiar voice froze her in her tracks.

She held her breath.

The voice continued. 'She's so young and horny; I can still feel her pussy gripping me, like a vice around my cock. God, it was hot. You'll love her.'

Bradford's voice. Breathless and weak, low and excited, but still his voice.

Simone knew he was talking about her. The certainty turned her insides into a writhing mass of fury and embarrassment.

She had no idea who he was talking to but it didn't matter. In that moment she longed for nothing more than to spit in his face.

Simone stomped around the corner formed by a tall stack of shelves.

Bradford leaned against the wall, eyes closed, trousers pooled around his ankles. One hand gripped his cock, once more thick and erect. The other hand held a mobile phone against his ear. His breathing hissed through the enclosed space, tight and raspy.

'Looks?' he murmured. 'Blonde. Great tits. Sexy little mouth and cute butt perfect for smacking.'

Simone stepped forward. 'You forgot to mention my face, arsehole.'

Bradford dropped the phone. His eyes flashed open. His mouth formed a wide, silent 'O'.

'Yeah, fucker. It's me.' All threat of tears vanished.

'Just a minute, I know what this must sound like but—'

'No, you don't. Well you probably do, but I don't care. Pull your trousers up, you pathetic pervert.'

The calm exterior vanished. In its place Bradford became a shrinking, nervous man with twitching hands and a shifting gaze. He tugged his trousers up and belted them into place. 'It's my wife,' he said.

Blindsided by the sharp subject change, Simone shook her head. 'What?'

'On the phone, my wife. Please— I think you should speak to her.'

Simone tapped her foot, caught off guard. It was the first time she'd ever heard him say the word 'please'. 'What the hell would I want to do that for? Everyone knows you hate your wife.'

He rolled his eyes. A little of his usual authority returned. 'Yes, everyone knows. Everyone *thinks* they know but my business is exactly that. *Mine.* Pick up the phone, Simone.'

Too angry to think, she grabbed the phone and pressed it to her ear. 'Who is this?'

'Dianne Bradford.' The voice on the other end of the phone was a female version of Bradford. 'You're Simone Daye?'

'Yes, and I want to know—'

'I'm talking right now. I understand you recently interviewed with my husband.'

She cut a glance at the man watching her through the gloom of the stationary cupboard. 'Interviewed? No, I don't think—'

'Fine, I understand you recently fucked my husband.' Impatience tightened her words.

She knows? What the fuck is this?

Bradford nodded at her.

'Um, yes, I did.'

'Did you like it?'

'Excuse me?'

Bradford plucked the phone from her grasp and murmured into the receiver. 'I'll handle this from here, dear. See you at dinner. Love you.' He hung up and tucked the phone into his pocket.

Long seconds passed before Simone spoke again. When she did, her voice emerged high and shrill, a squeak in the darkness. 'What the actual fuck?'

'My wife and I, despite the office gossip, are happily married and intend to stay that way.'

'So what the hell were you shagging me for?'

'Like she said, an interview.'

Simone tugged her hair. 'Make sense, will you?'

'My wife and I like to experiment.' Bradford smoothed invisible creases from his jacket. 'We invite willing men or women to join us a few times a month to keep our bedtime activities fresh.'

Silence.

From outside, Simone heard the burble of voices. The slam of a door. The gurgle overhead from water gushing through the piping as a toilet flushed three doors down.

'Fresh?'

'Swingers clubs are our usual choice but this month Dianne wanted me to find a woman at work. The idea of me . . .' he lowered his head.

'You what?'

'The thought of me fucking someone over my desk really turns her on. She begged me to do it. So I did.'

Simone slumped against one of the cabinets. 'You used me. You didn't want *me*; I was just a prop for your bloody wife!'

'And I was a quick pity-fuck you used after chasing down a gay man. Don't point fingers, Simone.'

He had a point.

Some of the righteous fire leaked from her voice. 'So what now? I failed your stupid interview. Do you find some other poor bimbo to hump against that massive desk?'

Bradford grinned. 'On the contrary, you passed with flying colours. You're an amazing lover, Simone. So responsive, so eager and deliciously free. When you let go, you enjoyed yourself as much as I did.'

His voice oozed that easy confidence again. Simone knew that to deny the facts would be churlish.

She looked him up and down. 'I passed. What does that mean?'

'It means I invite you to dinner this weekend. At my house. You'll meet Dianne and discuss if you'd like to take this game any further.'

'Dinner?'

'Yes, do you like fish?'

'I guess.'

'Good. I'll pick you up at 7 p.m. on Saturday. Wear something nice.' He turned to walk past her. She blustered after him. Grabbed his arm. When he dropped his gaze to her hand she jerked away.

'Wait a minute. You can't order me around like that. You can't just assume I have no plans. Who says I want to do this?'

'*Do* you have plans?'

A pause. Then a sullen shake of her head.

Bradford closed the small space between them and tucked his fingers beneath her chin. 'You do now. See you at 7 p.m. Saturday. Nice clothes.' He pushed a wad of damp lace in her palm. 'Wear those again. I like them.' Leaning down, he brushed a kiss against her cheek and walked away.

Seconds later, the door to the cupboard clicked open, then shut.

Simone blew a heavy breath through her mouth, flicking the handful of lace to reveal her knickers soaked from her juices and his.

Dirty old pervert.

She grinned.

MALCOLM

Malcolm leaned low over his soft drink, plagued by one worrying, persistent thought.

I'm over-dressed.

As if to highlight his discomfort, a round-bellied bald man stalked passed his table wearing nothing but a bright red thong and a bristling thatch of chest hair. He appeared comfortable and very much at home among the other scantily clad occupants of the fetish club.

Lucky him.

Malcolm returned to his drink and watched the ice cubes melt away. He fought back a sigh.

This was a stupid idea.

'Why so glum, pretty boy?' The voice came from directly in front. Soft. Female. Curious, though edged with something authoritative that made Malcolm's skin tingle.

A pair of sparkly heels stepped into view. Though he longed to lift his head, instead he clung to his coat and said nothing.

'Orange, blue or green?' she said.

I know that voice. It's her. It must be her.

For long moments Malcolm did nothing. His tongue cleaved to the roof of his mouth and butterflies the size of footballs thumped around his belly. He rolled back his sleeve to display the band of orange and white circling his wrist. A bead of sweat rolled down his spine beneath the coat. The lining clung to his skin.

'Oh, goodie. Look at me.'

He obeyed.

Blue eyes. Sharp as shards of sapphire. She had long black lashes, fluttering against her high cheekbones to leave long, spikey shadows. Her hair, held back with a black band, formed a long tail of golden strands down the back of her neck.

'You *are* a pretty boy,' she purred.

He shrugged and pressed his legs together beneath the table.

A frown. 'Don't you want to play? You shouldn't wear that band if you don't want people bothering you.' She stared at him.

Malcolm shifted on his seat. The weight of her gaze pressed on his chest and squeezed his lungs. He looked back to his coke.

'So . . . are you interested? I have a booth.'

Malcolm's breath burned in his throat. He longed to speak but the words wouldn't come. She was too close. Near enough that the heat of her body warmed his arm through the coat. Her breath tickled his hair.

'Jesus, do you speak? Are you in the right place?'

'Yes,' he managed.

'Then talk to me, would you?'

'This is my first time.'

Silence. It dragged on, and on some more until Malcolm felt sure he might burst.

'You're new?' The frown deepened. 'Fuck.'

A wave of shame boiled through his gut. He surged to his feet. 'I need to go.' Darting out from behind the table, he aimed for the door.

'No, wait. I'm so sorry.' The woman hurried after him. It looked like hard work in those heels.

Malcolm stopped. Peered down at her. For the first time he realised he was taller. Not that it made any difference. Her smile, her posture, the confident thrust of her shoulders and chin made him feel three inches high.

'Let's start again. I'm Christina.' She extended her hand.

'Malcolm.' When he took her cool, dry fingers into his, he was more aware than ever of the sticky sweat on his palms. He immediately wiped them on his jeans and picked up his glass once more.

'Malcolm. Good. Sorry. If I'd known you were new I wouldn't have come on so hard. You should have said something.'

'I couldn't, I—'

'Don't apologise. It's my fault. I should have known from your band.'

'It wasn't very visible.'

She nodded. 'Classic newbie error. Shall we just talk? Do you want a drink? Or . . . ?' Her gaze strayed back to his wristband. 'I'm looking for playmates too.' Her voice became a low whisper and she held out her wrist to display an orange band cut through with black stripes.

'Why is yours different?' Malcolm looked at the white lines running through his own band.

Christina grinned. 'I'm a dominant.'

The soft cries of a man two feet away, brought a distracting rush of heat to his face and neck. When Malcolm looked towards the sound he immediately wished he hadn't.

Christina followed his gaze. Laughed. 'Billy likes to be paddled. Don't let those girlie little screams worry you.'

Though his cheeks burned, Malcolm couldn't help but sneak another look. The man wriggled and cried out, his body tied over a wide, leather bench. His bare, pasty arse faced the ceiling. The man's backside darkened from white to pink, then a deep, rosy red as each impact of the heart-shaped paddle brought blood and heat surging to the surface.

Malcolm tightened his grip on the glass. 'I'm a bit out of my depth here.'

'I'll say.' Christina gave him a small smile. 'I think you'd better come with me.' She walked off without looking back.

Here we go . . .

Malcolm left his drink and scurried after her.

The chains and cuffs, though cold, were not uncomfortable. Malcolm tested their strength by pulling his wrists. He wasn't going anywhere.

Across from him, perched on a black leather stool, Christina sipped from a glass of water. She watched him, eyes bright and wide, intent on his face.

'How do you feel?'

'Okay.'

'Sure?'

'Yes. I like it.'

Malcolm's skin prickled. The hairs on his arms and the back of his neck lifted. He shifted for a better position, but couldn't find one with his hands tied behind his back. His jacket, removed at last, lay on the floor beneath his knees.

He still wore the black vest he'd arrived in, but not the jeans. Christina had coaxed him out of those mere minutes before. They made an untidy pile near her glittery shoes. He wore boxers, again in black and though he hadn't expected to show them off, his stomach clenched in relief. He doubted tighty-whities would impress this woman.

Christina put down her glass and stood. The motion took her face out of immediate view. Malcolm craned his neck. She stayed close. He tilted his head all the way back.

'Are you sure you're happy with this?' she whispered.

I've never been happier in my life.

Malcolm shrugged. 'I'm fine. I'd say if I wasn't.'

'Good. Then we're going to talk about safe words.'

'I know all about safe words. I—' He broke off. Watched the light of suspicion brighten in Christina's eyes.

'You said you were new.'

'I am.'

'So . . .'

Busted. Fuck.

His shoulders slumped. 'I suppose I should tell you.'

'Tell me what?' She stepped back, quick and agile in those four inch heels. She stood behind a stool. Waited.

'I'm not new. Well, I *am* new, but not *totally* new. I've been here before.'

'Go on.' Her voice deepened. Blue eyes narrowed.

Deep breath. 'I first came when my girlfriend dumped me. I was looking for someone else. Quickly.'

'A quick fuck?' Christina's lips tightened. Her hands curled into fists.

'Maybe. I saw you then. With a whip. You were laying into some guy and he was bawling like a six-year-old. You laughed at him. He said 'stop' – begging! – but you just kept lashing him. Then he said 'Bugs Bunny' and you stopped.'

Christina froze. She folded her arms. Then put them to her sides. Folded them again.

'He just needed a breather.' Malcolm rushed on, unsure what to do about the terrible stare directed his way. 'You didn't hurt him, he just— I don't know . . . got overwhelmed?'

'You're talking about Chester. He always uses cartoon characters for his safe words. I haven't seen him for a month.' She fussed with the ends of her hair, rubbing the side of her left shoe against the opposite calf. 'How long have you been watching me?'

'I'm sorry! I didn't know what I was doing. Vicki dumped me, wanking did nothing. I didn't know what to do. Then I came here and saw you. I felt better.'

'How long?' She glared, her body a study in tension.

'Just that one time. I swear. This is my first time since then. I hoped you'd be here but I didn't know for sure.'

'Why?'

'I wanted to talk to you.'

'Why?' Same word, utterly different question. Christina's voice softened and became wary with a hint of curiosity.

Don't make me say it. I feel like a pervert as it is, all tied up like this. Don't make me say it out loud.

'Why?' Softer still.

He studied the toes of her shoes. 'I wanted— I hoped that you would do me.' The words came out in a breathless rush, tumbling over each other like a barrel of bingo balls.

Christina stopped frowning. '*Do you?* How?'

He cringed but it didn't matter now. How much worse could it get? 'With the whip. Or a paddle. A flog. Anything. I don't care.'

Silence fell between them. Through it, Malcolm heard the occasional yelp or moan of pleasure. Their booth, though small and private boasted none of the fancy soundproofing some others had.

'You want me to dominate you.' Not a question.

'Yes.' He squirmed beneath her gaze. 'After I saw you that night I did some research. I've never seen anything like it. I watch as much porn as the next guy but some of those sites were crazy. Chains, cages, masks, gags and strap-ons . . .' Thinking of it set his heart pounding.

Her gaze swept up and down his body, settling on the growing tent in his boxers. 'You really get off on this.'

'Don't you?' He countered.

'Yes. But I don't normally 'do' strangers.'

'Then why approach me?'

She hesitated long enough that he feared she wouldn't answer. 'I like your face.'

Malcolm opened his mouth. Then closed it. 'Thanks. I think. I like you. What you did to that guy . . . excited me. I'm still excited.'

She looked again at his crotch. 'I'd say that's an understatement.'

He risked a smile. 'You're not freaked out?'

'Not any more. So you want to sub for me, like Chester?'

Malcolm raised himself on his knees. 'Yes. Please.'

'Did you see what I did to him? All of it?'

Malcolm swallowed a groan and shifted his knees to ease the ache warming his groin. 'I saw enough.'

'Really? Because everything I did to him, I'll do to you. Understand?'

'I want you to.'

She smiled, radiant and cheeky all at once. 'Safe words then: your 'stop' word is 'banana.' Your 'it's-nearly-too-much' word is 'almond.' Understand?'

'Yes.'

'Good. Then come here.'

Malcolm moved as if to stand. A loud cough stopped him dead.

'I didn't say stand, pretty boy.'

'So how do I . . . oh.' Malcolm steadied himself on his knees then tried an experimental shuffle. With his hands cuffed behind his back movement proved hard but possible. When he reached Christina, she spread her legs and gripped his head in both hands.

She kissed him on the nose, then each cheek before pressing his face deep into her chest.

The corset she wore lifted her breasts up and out. They were small, but the garment gave them incredible cleavage.

Malcolm inhaled the salty tang of sweat on her skin and something else. Vanilla. He took another deep breath, flicking out his tongue to taste her.

Seconds later, cool air rushed back into his face and his cheek throbbed with a stinging slap. Not hard, but enough to make him yelp.

'Did I say you could use your tongue on me?'

Malcolm tried to speak, but no words came. He looked up at Christina and knew he was wide eyed and open mouthed. 'No, but—'

'Then why did you?'

'I wanted to taste you.'

Her hand came down again, open palm, fingers bent back. His left cheek burned to match the right.

'You ask first. Same as Chester. Understand?'

'Okay, Jesus.'

'Excuse me?'

Malcolm hunched his shoulders. 'I mean, yes Christina.'

Another slap. He reeled and though she was careful not to catch him with her fingernails, Malcolm's face throbbed.

'Think, pretty boy.'

'Yes . . .' he gazed into her face, trying to read clues from the ice blue of her eyes. 'Mistress?'

Her glare melted away into a beaming smile. 'Much better. And that's how you'll address me in future. Well done.'

Her voice was sing-song and condescending. The pat on the head more so. Just the same, Malcolm's cock pressed against the front of his boxers and a shiver raced down his spine. He looked at the floor and tried to steady his mind and his body.

Christina leaned forward. Stroked his head. She pushed her fingers through his hair and held tight, pulling him back until he leaned far back over his ankles. His thighs and stomach strained with the effort to keep from toppling over.

'You like this, don't you? A little pain? Discomfort?'

'Yes, Mistress.'

'Good.' She let go and stalked away.

Malcolm righted himself and glanced at his boxers. The urge to grasp his erection made him dizzy.

'Can I ask a question, Mistress?'

'You may.'

He winced at the corrective tone. 'Are you— I mean, can we—?'

'Spit it out.'

'Is sex allowed here?'

'Penetrative? Yes. This is one of the few local clubs that does allow it.'

The news made Malcolm's cock throb. 'Can we? Do you want to?'

'I do have sex here sometimes. But not with strangers or first-timers.'

'Oh.' He looked at the floor.

'I'm not here to service anybody. "Playmates" doesn't mean "quick fuck", Malcolm. It means *mate*. A *friend* you play with when the mood takes you both. If you want that then we've got a long way to go.' Christina stalked closer. She did so slowly, careful to cross each foot across the other in an exaggerated cat-walk strut. It would have looked ridiculous if not for the heels and gleaming corset.

'I don't get involved with *rebounders*. After all, when you're done here you'll just find another girl willing to let you stick your hand in her pants.'

Malcolm tensed. 'It's not like that.'

'Really?' One arched eyebrow added all the extra emphasis the word lacked.

He sagged, knowing he was in danger of failing some bizarre test. With effort he drew his mind away from the ache in his boxers and tried to think.

Across the room someone called out 'Red' in a shrill, breathless voice. Hearing it reminded Malcolm of his own safe words.

He knew he could use them and end everything in an instant.

But he didn't want to.

When he next looked up, Malcolm made his voice strong, clear and steady.

'The women I know don't like this stuff. They think it's just for perverts. Why do you think I got dumped?'

A flicker of sympathy passed through her eyes. 'And what do *you* think?'

He licked his lips. 'It's another way of getting to know somebody. It takes a lot of trust to do what we're doing. There's nothing perverse about that.'

'You trust me?'

'I like you.' For the first time he felt comfortable saying it. He met her gaze and held it, willing her, silently begging her to see the truth.

'You don't know me.'

'I want to. Besides, you don't know me either.'

She tossed her head. 'No, but I'm the one in charge.'

'No, you're not.'

Christina held his gaze. Something in her shoulders and back relaxed. She nodded slowly. 'Are you sure you're new?'

'Yes. Promise. But I *have* done research. I've been reading blogs and chatting on forums. The submissive is the one with the real power.'

'Not many people see it that way.'

He shrugged. Or tried to with his hands bound. 'I do.'

'No sex today, Malcolm. I mean that.' Though her tone remained stern, Christina looked away. She fussed with the end of her ponytail again. Tugged on the cords of her corset. 'I don't get what you want from me. What is it you think I can give you?'

'Freedom.' At her bemused tilt of the head, Malcolm pressed on. 'I'm freer with someone else in charge. And I don't want to be hurt exactly, but . . .' His cock began to tingle again. 'I want you to tell me what to do. Tie me

up. Paddle me. Even . . .' The warmth rushed into his face and stayed there.
'What?'

Gazing at this woman he met a mere hour ago, Malcolm took a deep breath and said the words he'd only voiced in his private fantasies. 'I want you to fuck me with a strap-on.'

Delight filled Christina's features. 'We're going to get on just fine. Don't move.' She left the booth.

Malcolm stayed put, gazing into the middle distance.

When the strain from his tied hands began to tell on his shoulders, he whimpered and sat back on his heels.

He had no way to tell time in the small, red space. Only the occasional murmur of conversation from beyond the door and the sharp shriek of someone enjoying impact play let him know there were other people around. He imagined what it would be like to feel the lash of a whip against his back and shoulders. The heavy thud of a paddle against his rear.

The thought made his cock twitch again. He twisted his hips from side to side, seeking friction from the fabric of his boxers. He was still fidgeting when Christina returned.

'Stop that,' she said, hooking one hand beneath his arm to help him stand. 'The paddle bench is free. We're going to use it.'

Though he thought he knew what she meant, Malcolm gave a little whimper when he saw the bench. He froze, erection wilting within his boxers. 'Oh, God.'

The black, leather monstrosity stood five feet high with padded foot and arm rests at the front and back. Shiny silver loops and hooks protruded from all four corners. Long lengths of chain dangled from the back.

Malcolm eyed the contraption and edged closer to Christina. 'Wow.'

'Beautiful, isn't it?' She picked up one of the chains and let it fall. It slapped against the frame with a metallic clatter, a kinky percussion to her words. 'Lady Davina had it commissioned when this place was refurbed. It's set into the floor and has three more pieces that attach to the sides and back so you can spank four people at once.'

A glance around the wide space showed other less impressive, but no less intimidating play equipment. Large, plush sofas lined the walls, most filled with people quietly chatting.

Malcolm frowned. 'We're going to use it now? As in right now?'

'Problem?'

'What about all these people?'

'What about them?'

He looked around. 'Won't they mind?'

Christina smirked. 'There *are* private rooms, but if you're out here you expect to see a little of someone else's play. They know that. Using the equipment in these rooms also signals that you don't mind an audience.'

She turned to face him fully. '*Do* you mind an audience?'

Malcolm knew that wasn't all she meant. He looked away, searching the room for answers.

A woman, naked but for a tiny pink thong, stood strapped face down to a St Andrew's cross. Her limbs pulled outwards and formed a giant X against which a small man in leather shorts slapped the tails of a black, fluffy flogger.

Another corner, another frame, this one large and square, four chains hanging from the topmost corners. Between these chains stretched a leather swing, cradling another woman, this one utterly naked. Two men pinned her legs above her head. A third man knelt between her spread legs and gently inserted a narrow, blue vibrator. The woman tossed her head and moaned, a sound that carried across the room.

'Well?' Christina touched his arm.

Malcolm blew a heavy breath through his mouth. 'I doubt anybody's going to be watching us.'

'But they might, so this is important. Do you mind?'

'No . . . Mistress.'

'Good. Then on you get.' Christina patted a wider shelf on the padded table with a distinct groove down the middle.

Malcolm knelt on the cushioned outcrop and fed his arms through the gaps at shoulder height.

Humming, Christina walked around him, securing leather straps around his wrists, and then his ankles. A fifth, larger strap curved around his waist and trapped him in place.

'Nice,' she whispered. 'How do you feel?'

'Secure.'

'Good. Not wobbly or unstable?'

'No.'

'Safe?' Another loaded question.

'I'm fine.'

She nodded and stepped out of sight.

Though he craned his neck, the straps on the table prevented him from moving far in any direction. He caught a glimpse of her long blonde hair before she moved closer again.

'I'll use one of my softest floggers,' she said. 'Not too stingy, light on the skin. I'm going to hit you with it and you need to tell me how much it hurts on a scale of one to ten. One being 'not at all' and ten being 'holy fuck, I'm going to die.' Can you do that?'

He chuckled. 'I doubt you can hit me that hard.'

'Really?'

Malcolm heard the shift in Christina's tone and knew at once his words would cost him.

A *swishing* sound. He braced himself just as the lash of the tails caught him across the shoulder blades. 'Fuck!'

'Well?'

'Um . . . I don't know. Five?'

'Oh.' She laughed. 'I'd better reel it in a bit. Again.'

Another lash. Another yelp.

'Okay, more like two. Three. No, two.'

'Good.'

The next strike made Malcolm jerk against the restraints. 'Eight. That's an eight.'

When Christina walked back into view, her breasts heaved. A gleam filled her eyes and a cute, pink flush washed across her neck and chest. She grinned, tucked the handle of the flogger into the side of her knickers and crossed her arms. 'That's a warm up. We're going to have fun now. Remember; 'banana' and 'almond'.'

'Why those words?'

She shrugged. 'How likely are you to use them in conversation tonight?'

'Not very.'

'So when I hear them, I know you mean it. Clear?'

Malcolm nodded.

Licking his dry lips he watched Christina walk out of sight once more.

He made fists, forcing his body to relax against the soft padding all around him. That done, he closed his eyes, letting himself drift on the sounds around him. He sought the subtle swish meaning Christina had pulled back her arm for another swing.

The first blow still caught him off guard.

More a stroke than a real impact. A gentle brushing of fluffy strands over his shoulders and across the top of his back. Without leaving his skin, the tails slithered over his spine and passed his tail bone, gliding over his boxers and then his thighs and calves.

A shudder rippled through his body, following the path of the flogger.

'That's nice,' he whispered.

A sound that might have been a smirk came from near his left ear. 'Good.'

The flogger came down again, across the backs of his thighs this time and Malcolm twitched against the frame.

The strikes continued in this fashion for a few minutes, light, teasing brushes, touches with long gaps in between that left his skin tingling in the cool air.

Then, just as he began to fall into the rhythm of it, the tails cracked down against his right shoulder, a stinging blow that made his eyes fly open. Before he could make a note of it, a matching impact cracked against his left shoulder. Then the right. Left again.

He moaned, twisting his wrists in the restraints as the strikes continued.

Not hard . . . they were no more than 'fours' on his self-generated scale, but they came so fast. With no recovery gap in between, the sensitivity climbed steadily.

Within six more strikes what was once a 'four' felt more like a 'seven' and he toyed with the idea of calling 'almond.'

Before he could speak the flogger began to travel again. Down his body, teasing the skin all over his back with quick-fire strikes.

Malcolm allowed his forehead to rest on the padded slab before him. With his fists clenched, he gritted his teeth and tried to understand what he felt. Not pain exactly, though that was certainly part of it, but a curious blend of that mixed with something else he couldn't pin point.

From the corner of his eye he saw the woman in the swing finally sit up. She kissed one of the three men clustered about her and hopped down. Though the men stayed close she paid no attention to them. Instead her gaze fixed on Malcolm. She smiled.

A particularly solid strike against his rear made him yelp like a spanked child. He jerked against the restraints, but could do no more than twist from side to side.

'How you doing, Malcolm?' Christina's voice seemed to come from miles away, edged with laughter.

'It's good.'

And, strange though it was, he knew it was true. The heat began to spread through his body and the air, once cold, now formed a welcome respite to the heat in his skin. The impacts against his backside increased, even through the barrier of his boxers. Soon the gentle warmth became a burn.

'Fuck,' he whispered.

Then it stopped. All of it.

Footsteps. Thunderous in the sudden still.

Malcolm became aware of his breathing, sweat-soaked skin and the roaring hardness of his cock pressed against the padded frame.

Then Christina walked back into view and all rational thought died. Her corset was gone. Knickers too. She stood before him beautiful and naked but for the glittery high heels.

'You said you wanted to lick me.' She quirked an eyebrow.

'Yeah?' He fought to moisten his mouth enough to allow coherent speech. 'I mean yes, Mistress. I really, *really* do.'

She hesitated. 'This . . . is strange for a first timer. Do you still feel safe?'

I feel amazing.

'God, yes, Mistress.'

'Do you need—'

'I'm fine.' He growled, frustration and longing getting the better of him.

'Please Christi— Mistress. Just tell me what to do.'

She nodded. 'Lick me.' In one graceful stride, she stepped on to a padded shelf that put her hips level with his face. In one hand she held a palm-sized square of thin, clear material which she draped over the bald, slick lips between her legs.

Malcolm frowned. 'What the hell is that?'

She rolled her eyes. 'A dental dam. Just think of it as a condom for female oral.'

He should have been grateful. Part of him knew that. The rest of him reeled as he caught the musky scent drifting from between Christina's slim, pale thighs. In that moment nothing mattered more than touching her. Feeling her delicate bud swell beneath his tongue.

She pressed her hips forward.

He put out his tongue.

'That's it, pretty boy. Lick me.' Her voice, so husky and deep brought an additional thrill Malcolm didn't see coming. He moaned and pushed his tongue past her outer lips.

The skin about his bound wrists and ankles tingled insistently. He tugged against the restraints, not to escape, but to feel them dig into his flesh. The reminder of his impaired movement thrilled him. Knowing that he would be there until Christina chose to release him made his cock ache. His imagination raced through a dozen scenarios, each involving restraints and pleasure giving.

Malcolm projected his eager thoughts into the motions of his lips and tongue.

'Careful.' Her voice took on a breathy quality. 'It's only latex. Don't put a hole in it.'

It took Malcolm long seconds to realise she meant the dental dam. He returned to licking up and down the front of her slit and along her inner lips.

She moaned and bucked against his face. The whole time she kept one hand pressed to the back of his head. He couldn't move. Even if he wanted to.

'Now,' she murmured. 'Count.'

Malcolm felt the lash of the flog again. It hit him across the back, a firm 'five'. He yelped and pulled his lips free long enough to cry out. 'One!'

'Good. Keep going.'

She lashed him again, four strikes in quick succession that he dutifully pulled his head free to count.

Then again.

And again.

At fifteen strikes of the flog, Malcolm had to pull his head back. He licked his lips and swallowed.

'I didn't say stop.' Christina's voice held an edge.

'It's hard. I can't concentrate.'

'I know. That's what makes it fun. And I should mention, if you lose count, I start all over again. I'm trying to get to a specific number.'

He shuddered at the thought of more punishment. 'What number?'

'I'll tell you when we get there. Lick.'

The order sent a pleasurable surge through Malcolm's body. His cock swelled, balls full and tight between his legs. Sweat beaded on his upper lip. Twisting and bucking his hips did nothing while the promise of release so tantalisingly close made him grunt in frustration. He teetered on the edge, just too far away to tip himself over.

'Please,' he whispered.

'"Please" what?'

'I need . . .' He knocked his forehead against the padded frame.

Christina stopped flogging his back long enough to peer at him. 'Don't be afraid to ask for what you want. You might not get it but if you don't ask you never will.'

Embarrassment tied his stomach in knots. But he had no choice. His erection ached so much he could barely think. 'I need to come.'

Christina smiled. 'You will. Trust me.'

'Soon?'

'Maybe.' She swatted his shoulders with the flogger. 'But you have to make me come before you do.'

He grunted. 'Thirty-six.'

'Very good. I mean it by the way. Make me come all over your pretty little face.'

The flogging resumed and Malcolm returned his lips to Christina's pussy.

She was wet now; he could see the glistening fluid beneath the dental dam. Saliva glistened on his side of the latex which made a faint squelching sound each time she moved.

The sound of it, though strange at first, took on an erotic quality which matched the rhythmic *swish-flick* of the flog tails. Over and over they went and Malcolm counted each one. But they were harder now. Creeping from 'fours' to persistent 'sixes.' Then 'sevens.'

He clenched his fists, desperate to keep going.

She wants to come. I want her to come. That's all I want. I can do it – I'll make her cream all over my face.

That thought, more than any other, gave him the will to push through the growing pain. His pleasure hinged on hers and that made him desperate to satisfy. Nothing mattered more than making his new mistress gush all over his lips and chin.

He craned forward, pushing his tongue out. Leaving the slick sides of her pussy lips he ventured deeper. Harder. Faster.

She tensed. Gripped his hair with one hand.

The tails of the flogger fell over his face, temporarily blinding him. Malcolm didn't care.

She trembled beneath his ministrations and the sound of his tongue diving in and out of her moist crevice formed orchestral music to his ears.

Christina's hand tightened in his hair and she pulled, grinding against his face and groaning, long and loud.

Her release sent tremors through her whole body and Malcolm strained his fingers to stroke what he could reach of her hips. For long seconds she stood pressed against him, body shaking, chest heaving, slowly drifting back from whatever wonderful journey her orgasm took her on.

When the tails of the flogger slithered over his back Malcolm released a low breath. 'Forty-one.'

Pulling back, Christina laughed and shook her head. 'Did you lose count somewhere?'

'What? No, forty-one.'

Another shake. 'Forty-two. It is the answer to everything. Looks like I'll have to start again.'

Malcolm gaped. His super sensitive back and shoulders throbbed at the suggestion of more punishment, but his tender cock responded with an eager jerk as he marvelled at finding a Douglas Adams fan in a fetish club. 'But— I counted. I'm sure of it.'

'Did you count the one to your face?'

Understanding dawned. 'I thought you were resting your arm.'

She chuckled. 'Don't worry. It will be worth it. Wait there. Have a breather.' Still laughing, Christina stepped out of his line of sight.

Malcolm waited, staring blankly across the room.

His entire body sang with pleasure. Every muscle coiled tight and ready to snap. Between his legs, the neglected length of his cock pulsed and throbbed.

So hard . . .

The slightest touch would tip him over. Heat gathered low in his belly and threatened to consume him at any moment. He licked his lips but his dry tongue made little difference.

The woman from the sling caught his eye again. She smiled and, without breaking eye contact, sank to her knees beside the three men watching her. One grabbed her hair and pulled. She opened her mouth, eagerly accepting the fat, stiff cock shoved between her lips.

'Want some of that do you?' Christina's voice snapped him back to attention.

'I—'

'Don't worry, pretty boy, I'll look after you.'

Deft hands grabbed the waistband of his boxers and tugged them down to his knees. Cool air caressed his aching balls and cock. He moaned.

'I promised you'd come tonight and I always keep my promises. Can you keep yours?'

Swissssh.

He closed his eyes. 'One.'

'Good boy.'

And she began again, swatting with light, rhythmic touches that seemed all about wrist action and little more.

Malcolm dutifully counted, struggling to ignore the burn across his rear cheeks. The flogger rarely landed anywhere else now, except for an occasional swipe against his bulging balls when an over enthusiastic swat curled the tails beneath him.

At thirty-seven, a long line of sweat ran into his eyes. He trembled and the silver buckles around his wrists and ankles rattled against the frame.

'Fuck,' he cried as his hips bucked to escape the blows. But there was nowhere to go.

'What was that, pretty boy?'

Swisssh.

'Thirty-eight. I can't do much more of this. My cock is—'

Swisssh, swisssh.

Oh, good-fucking-God!

'Count, Malcolm. Don't whimper like a baby.'

'Forty.'

Swissh.

Fuck!

'I can't hear you!'

'Forty-one,' he bellowed.

A giddy sense of pride swelled within him. Pleasure at counting this far. Pride that Christina had no reason to be disappointed. Surprise and glee at having finally found what he wanted. What he needed.

The next impact of the flogger missed his rear entirely.

Malcolm shrieked and jerked at the restraints as the tails whipped round and struck the base of his super-sensitive cock. He scrunched his eyes shut. 'Forty-two. Sweet, holy-fucking-Christ, forty-two. Forty-two!'

'Well done, pretty boy.' Christina stepped back into his field of view and grabbed his trembling cock.

He moaned again, thrusting against her fingers which were cool and slick. She stroked him up and down, her grip firm. The touch of her fingers dragged a low growl from deep in his gut and Malcolm tensed. Squeezed his eyes shut.

His orgasm rolled in like a freight train and flattened everything. Winking stars of gold and silver exploded across his vision. Release squeezed his agonised balls until his load boiled free and streamed into the air. He gasped. It seemed to have no end. On and on until Christina's hand gleamed with the sticky, white deposit. And more came until Malcolm's moans trailed away into soft whimpers.

The last strike against his arse caught him completely off guard.

Not the sharp, half-stroking slap of the flogger, but Christina's flat palm. She slapped him once and held her hand in place, digging in with her nails.

He felt sure he might die from the pleasure.

When the orgasm waned he sagged against the restraints, panting like a winded horse.

'Okay, pretty boy. We're done.'

He tried to lift his head. The effort cost too much.

'Malcolm? Hello?'

He had fuzzy thoughts of moving. Or maybe opening his eyes. But he couldn't. Instead, he enjoyed the incredible afterglow of his best and most satisfying orgasm in weeks. The little aftershocks of it still flowed through his body occasionally making his fingers twitch.

The dizzy bliss ended when the padded shelf beneath his knees abruptly vanished. At the same time, something near his wrists clicked and loosened. He fell.

His eyes jerked open. 'Fuck!'

'Malcolm!' Christina's face appeared above him, her expression one of panic. 'Are you okay?'

'Why am I on the floor?'

'Are you okay?' she insisted.

'Yes, yes, I'm fine. What the hell just happened?'

She dropped to her knees, toying with the end of her ponytail. 'Don't do that to me.'

He gave her a blank stare.

'I thought you'd passed out. You can't just— you have to answer me after a scene like that! How else will I know you're okay?'

'How did you do that?'

She bit her lip. 'All of the equipment has a quick release. In case something goes wrong. Like if someone panics or gets hurt. This frame has a switch that releases all the restraints.'

'And dumps you on the floor?'

She gave a sheepish shrug. 'Normally someone else would be there— they could catch you. Oh, man. I've never seen someone do that. I've heard of it but I've never been the cause.'

Malcolm rolled over, suddenly aware that his naked, wilting cock was visible to the entire room. 'I don't get it.'

'You went away. Not quite *sub-space*, but . . . pleasure overload? I thought I'd knocked you out.'

I'll say "pleasure overload". Wow . . .

'Talk to me, next time, okay?'

His heart gave a little skip. 'Next time?'

A shy smile. 'Get up so we can clean you off.'

A glance around the room showed groups and couples so involved with their own fun that no one paid Malcolm and his naked rear a second glance. None but one man, dressed in what appeared to be a pair of belts. He loitered nearby huffing and drumming his fingers against his crossed arms.

'You guys done?' he snapped.

'Yes, sorry.' Christina leapt forward to wipe down the frame. She looked smaller now, somehow more frail, struggling to unfasten the buckles. Malcolm helped, holding the frame while she slipped the loops free. 'There, all yours.'

'Cheers.' Belt-Man nodded and began to rearrange the restraints. A short distance away, another man in a leather mask and nothing else, waited with his arms linked behind his back.

Malcolm followed Christina back to her booth. He slumped onto the seat, then leapt up with a yelp when the sensitive skin of his arse reminded him of the last half hour. 'I won't be able to sit for days.'

Grinning, Christina handed him a bottle of water. 'You'll be fine. Trust me, by tomorrow you'll forget it ever happened.'

'I doubt that.' He drank half the contents without pausing for breath, smacking his lips before glugging the remainder.

'You should sip that you know. You're not used to it.'

'I feel like I've run a bloody marathon.'

'It can be like that. But you *will* get used to it. You'll learn how to control what your body does and how to deal with it. Practise. Same as everything else.' She sipped from her own water bottle, tucking a few stray wisps of hair behind her ear.

Malcolm gazed at her. 'Thank you.'

'For whipping you silly and giving you a hand job?'

'Wow. You Domme types can be pretty blunt.'

Christina gave him a level stare. 'Some more than others. It works for me. Did you like it?'

'The bluntness? I suppose so, but I don't think—'

'No, the frame. The flog. Did you like me dominating you? Hurting you?'

'Oh,' Though it seemed silly at this point, Malcolm's neck and face warmed. 'It was amazing. That's what I was thanking you for. I've never done anything like that. It felt so . . .'

'Painful?'

'Perfect. Vicki and I were good together – to start with – but there was always something missing. I didn't know what until tonight.'

Christina peeled the label off her water bottle. 'Good.'

Malcolm bit his lip. 'Look, I'm not asking you to date me or anything stupid like that. We just met and I don't know how it works outside this building. But I *do* know I want to do that again. With you.'

Christina stopped playing with her water. She gazed at the shredded label before balling up the pieces and poking them into the neck of the bottle. 'I don't know . . .'

'Hey,' he reached for her hand, changed his mind and let his fingers lie on the table. 'I don't know what this involves – contracts and agreements or whatever – but that's not what I mean. Yes, I want to do it again, but mostly I want to talk to you. Learn stuff.'

She frowned. 'Contracts?'

'Like that book?'

Christina rolled her eyes and shoved the bottle aside. 'Well, first of all, if we're going to have anything else to do with each other, put that nonsense out of your head. That's not how I work. Some people – perhaps – but not me.'

'Oh.' Malcolm's flush finished climbing his neck and cheeks and ended its journey across his forehead. 'Sorry. I just—'

'Did what a lot of other people have done.' She softened. 'But you've also done stuff that people *don't* do, which is follow up with actual research.'

He shuffled his fingers on the table top. 'So what now?'

'How about you come with me to a munch?'

'Now?' Malcolm looked over his shoulder, trying to find a clock. 'It's it a bit late.'

Christina laughed. The gesture smoothed some of the lines from her forehead. It made her seem younger. 'Not food – well, there might be food – I mean a social gathering. They're called "munches." The next one is at The King's Arms on Sunday. A group of people from the kink scene get together and chat.'

His hesitancy must have shown in his face because Christina patted his hand.

'Just a chat, I promise. We'll grab a drink or two and talk about what we do. What we like.'

'Sex-wise?'

'No, just normal, vanilla stuff. Like films and books and music. Let's see if we're compatible. And who knows? Maybe we'll find more we like about each other.'

Malcolm grinned, staring into Christina's bright, lively eyes and knowing, at last, that he'd done the right thing. 'Yes, thanks. I'd like that.'

READ ON FOR A FREE
BONUS STORY

LARA

When I entered the coffee shop, I knew it was going to be a good day.

Vicki looked amazing. She had a pretty little red scarf wrapped around her head and big silver earrings shaped like spirals. With a wide smile on her lips, she was the very definition of beauty. I dumped my bag on the floor and squished in beside her.

Two slices of lemon cheesecake sat on the table, beside a pair of lattes. 'For me?'

'No, I'm just really hungry today.' With a grin and a teasing glint to her dark eyes, she nudged one of the plates towards me. 'Lemon swirl, extra cream and one chai latte.'

I could have kissed her.

'Thank you! I've had the worst morning.' Stabbing a fork at the narrow end, I hiked a piece of cheesecake to my mouth. A burst of sweet biscuit cut through the tart tang of lemon. 'We had an accident on the ward.'

Vicki touched the side of her mouth. 'Was anybody hurt?'

'No more than they already were.' I continued over her confused look. 'I'm on fractures this week. The kid who fell already had a broken leg. He didn't make it worse, but it must have hurt. Poor sod. I held him for half an hour while he cried for his mum.'

The memory still gave me chills. Fortunately, the warm press of Vicki's arm against mine formed a suitable distraction. 'Are you coming to mine tonight?'

Vicki grinned. 'Sure. I'll bring wine.'

'Great, that takes us up to four bottles.'

'I'll bring two then.' She laughed. I joined her, more from the joy of watching her laugh than the idea of getting drunk. Though that wasn't a bad idea either. We *both* relaxed more with a little alcohol inside us.

A little bubble of warmth grew in my belly.

'Will Shannon be there?'

I looked away. Cleared my throat. 'No, I— we broke up.'

'Lara, really? When?' Vicki sat forward in her chair, shoving the cheesecake to one side.

I diverted with a slurp of latte. How could I talk about it? With *her* of all people? When the heat of her gaze became too much I put the mug down and picked at a broken fingernail. 'Last week. We weren't working out. She wanted to see other people. I want to see other people . . .' I caught her staring at me, expression full of pity. It didn't help. Nor did her gentle pat to the back of my hand.

'Honey, I'm so sorry. I thought you two were doing great. I thought you looked good together.'

'Really?'

A flicker of hesitation. 'Yes. Like a pair of red headed super-models.'

The roundabout compliment lifted my spirits a fraction but it didn't change the truth I'd discovered about Shannon.

She's not the one I want.

I shrugged. 'Good looks aside, she was on the rebound. We both were. Rebound relationships don't last.'

Vicki rolled her eyes. 'If you'd stick with somebody for longer than a month you'd have less of a rebound problem. Are you working your way through the female population until someone sticks?'

I forced a laugh.

'Seriously, Lara, pick a girl, settle down and we'll all be happier for it.'

We?

Something heavy hit the side of our table. My latte toppled and sent a wave of milky liquid into my lap. I leapt up, squealing as it soaked my uniform. 'Hot, hot, hot!' My jump took me straight into the arms of the man behind me, tall and long haired with wet, brown eyes and a weak chin. His own drink wobbled but remained upright.

Tea dripped into my shoes. 'Watch what you're doing, will you?'

'I- I'm so sorry!' he stammered.

'Sorry doesn't help my uniform.'

'Lara, chill. It's just tea.' Vicki was beside me in an instant, dabbing my thighs with wads of tissues.

I held my breath. So close. As she bent to pat me dry, a shaft of sunlight speared through the window and caught the little silver beads she wore in her hair. I could smell her. Cocoa butter, lemon and cinnamon. Her hand moved higher up my dress, patting my hips, my stomach. The back of her wrist brushed my breast.

Oh, Jesus.

The floor seemed to dip and pitch beneath me. My knees buckled.

The man caught my arm. 'Are you okay?'

'I'm fine.' I stepped away from him. From Vicki soft hands. Chai latte puddled beneath me. 'I need the bathroom.' I ran before either of them could say speak, a quick slalom through the maze of tables to reach the rest rooms at the back. Inside, I slammed the door and dived into a cubical, leaning against the flimsy plywood divide.

My pulse filled my ears, the hot rush of blood through my veins like the crashing of waves. When I pressed my hands to my face, I realised they were shaking.

I can't do much more of this. I'll go mad.

Deep breath in. Another out. I forced myself to repeat the pattern, over and over until my heart steadied and the world ceased to spin. At last I could see clearly. The filthy, cracked seat on the toilet. The clumps of damp toilet tissue forming trails on the floor. The open tampon bin.

Out of the cubicle and up to the sinks. I caught my reflection in curved spout of the hand dryer, bulging, distorted eyes wide beneath a curtain of red hair riddled with split-ends. I pulled the silky strands off my face. *Too long.* The shade of devil-red far too bright. *Damn it, my roots are coming through. Is that a grey?* I should have cut it months ago – I nearly did – but Vicki liked long hair. I remembered her sad expression as she trailed her fingers through the long strands the day we walked to the salon. How she picked a long curl off my face and tucked it behind my ear.

I hadn't cut it since.

Through the closed door I heard the sounds of the coffee shop as it continued running without me. The hiss of industrial kettles, the harsh clank of percolators slammed against the bin, dumping used coffee grounds into teeming black bags.

'Enough,' I told my reflection. 'Go back out there and tell her the truth. Tell her why Shannon is no good.'

Encouraged by my pep talk I filled one of the sinks with warm water, swilling in a few squirts of handwash. Though awkward, washing the worst of the tea from my uniform took five minutes. Afterwards I stood beneath the hand dryer, to blow out the moisture.

The whole time I thought about what I would say. How I would say it. So many variations:

'I'm not with Shannon any more because she knew I was into someone else.'

Too vague.

'Shannon dumped my arse because she got fed up of playing second fiddle to another woman.'

Better – and true – but still not enough.

'Shannon dumped me because she knew I wanted you and was sick of watching me pine over you like a love-struck teenager.'

Bingo.

I dabbed my uniform with a clump of tissue. It wasn't going to get any better than that. No more excuses to stall. A glance in the mirror, adjusting a few strands of hair around my cheeks and pulling the rest into a ponytail.

I can do this.

Deep breath. Back outside.

When I reached the table the puddle was gone. In its place stood a black and yellow sign reading: *Caution. Wet Floor.*

I shifted it to one side.

Vicki stood to meet me. 'You were ages! Are you okay?'

'Fine. I just needed to clean my uniform. I don't have a spare on the ward.'

She shook her head. 'Now lunch is nearly over.'

'I know, I'm sorry. I freaked out. What was with that guy? Clumsy idiot.'

A small, excited giggle burst from Vicki's lips. I stared at her.

'Sorry.' Another giggle. 'But Malcolm's actually really sweet. He's getting you another drink.'

She knows his name?

My plan was crumbling. A glance at the clock told me I had five minutes to return to the ward and my tongue refused to form words. My entire mouth felt lined with sand and all the throat clearing in the world did nothing to help.

The stranger returned. 'Sorry about that. I didn't see the bag on the floor. Are you hurt?'

'What?' I licked my lips. The words made sense. I knew they did. But still, I couldn't speak. Instead, I stared at him like a deaf, mute idiot and wondered why Vicki was grinning so hard.

He touched my arm. 'Did the tea burn you?'

That woke me up. Sliding away from his fingers, I shook my head. 'No. You know what it's like in these places; all froth, no actual tea.'

He chuckled, a rich, jolly sound.

I hated it.

'This is for you.' He held out a blue and white takeaway cup.

'You didn't have to—'

'No, I insist. I'm clumsy and I ruined your lunch.'

'You didn't ruin my lunch.' Vicki's voice cut between us, low and seductive. Her smile widened.

Horror iced my insides. That expression— I knew it. I'd seen it before. In clubs. In pubs. With her last boyfriend.

No . . . no fucking way.

Malcolm chuckled and ran a hand through his hair. It was long in back, short in front, a classic mullet not popular since the years well before any of us were born.

I longed to punch him. Instead I took the cup and slammed it on the table. 'Well, thanks. I guess. Don't let us keep you.'

'You're not keeping me.' He didn't even look at me. Focused on Vicki, he grinned at her, all goofy teeth and thin lips. 'So, I'll see you later, Victoria?'

Victoria? Who the hell does he think he is?

'Sure.' Breathless, Vicki garbled her words in her haste to agree. She retrieved a black jacket from my seat and passed it to him. Her fingers lingered on the leather. 'Great. See you at eight.'

'Eight. Until then.' He glanced at me. 'Nice to meet you, Lara. Sorry about the drink.' He left the coffee shop, shrugging his big, gorilla arms into the jacket as he went.

Vicki watched him until he slipped out of view, eyes wide, lips slightly parted. She sat with a thump. 'Wow.'

'Wow?' I cried, wiping down my seat. 'Wow, what? Wow, what big, stupid teeth he's got?'

'No, come on, Lara, how hot was he?'

I glared at the space in the window I'd last seen him. 'If you like 70s footballer chic.'

Vicki fussed with her hair. 'Stop it. I know he's not your type, but believe me, he's buff.'

'Buff?' I squeezed the word through a throat suddenly tight and dry. 'No, he's not buff, he's horrible. Did you see that jacket? And what sort of klutz trips over a bag? It wasn't even moving.'

'You did dump it right in the path to the door.' She ignored my impotent splutterings and continued. 'He's so nice. And funny. You should have heard him while you were in the bathroom.'

'Sorry, too busy cleaning spilt tea off my clothes.' The fresh chai latte sat before me, mocking me. I froze. Sat straight. 'Did you say you'd see him at eight?'

For the first time since Malcolm's arrival Vicki met my gaze properly. A faint flush coloured her dark skin. Her eyes sparkled with pleasure. 'Yes. Sorry. I just— he asked and it slipped out. I couldn't take it back.'

'What slipped out?'

She squealed, unable to contain her glee. 'He asked me out.'

I couldn't breathe. The air seemed close, heavy on my chest. My plans whirled through my head, each carefully constructed sentence playing over and over on a loop I would never be able to speak out loud. 'But . . .' I gripped the arms of the chair. 'It was my drink he spilled.'

'Oh, come on, you don't even like guys.'

'I know, but—'

'I know we were supposed to watch movies, but we do that every week.'

I stared at her face. The face I wanted to cup gently in my palm while I kissed those full lips. I leaned back in my chair. Scratched at a stain on the leatherette.

'You're upset,' she whispered.

'No, I . . .' but I couldn't drum up a suitable lie.

'How about we do movies tomorrow instead? I'll bring three bottles of wine and you can open that bag of chocolate you've been hiding. And the tub of cookie dough ice cream. We'll pig out and I can tell you about my date.'

Though I felt my head move, I had no control over the nodding motion it performed.

'Lara?' Vicki touched my arm. 'Don't make me feel bad about this. It's just one night.'

I sighed. Smiled.

'Don't feel bad, Vic. It's about time you met someone nice.'

She beamed and the expression brightened her entire face. 'Thank you, I knew you'd understand.' She stood, grabbing her bag and coat while stuffing the last of her cheesecake into her mouth with the other hand. Crumbs sprayed the table. 'Gotta go. I'm late, but I'll call later.' She swallowed and gave another of those giggles. 'You've got to help me pick something to wear. Bye!' She darted out of the coffee shop.

The red scarf around her hair fluttered in the breeze, a thin, red banner that marked her trail until she slipped out of sight.

A WORD FROM THE AUTHOR

Hi guys. I'm Raven ShadowHawk and I'd like to personally thank you for buying this book. It means a great deal to me and ensures that every release that follows is better than the last as your money gives me the time and financial resources to make each publication the best it can be.

If you liked the book I'd really appreciate if you left a review for it.

As an independent author, I rely heavily on your reviews to spread the word about my work and encourage others to take a chance on me, just like you have done. If you like my stories, other people may too.

If you really, really liked the book (wheey-hey!) then perhaps you'd like to sign up for my newsletter? I send it once a quarter and pack it with news about upcoming projects, appearances and the odd free story. I also enter all subscribers into a free draw, gifting one subscriber my latest book each time I publish something new. Sign up today, join me between the sheets!

http://eepurl.com/0yKNj

OTHER TITLES BY RAVEN SHADOWHAWK

Slippers & Chains: Sugar Dust

Dan loves submissive women and longs to build a harem of willing females to fill what he lovingly calls his 'Slave Library.' He shares his plans for sexual bliss with Karen, the first of his submissives in his mind and his heart. But when an unexpected visit from his mother leads to uncomfortable questions about his ex, Dan realizes that past mistakes are catching up to him, faster than he can run.

The first D/s relationship to blend comfortably with her vanilla life is the one Karen shares with Dan. She treasures the freedom in the act of submission and wants nothing more than to share it with her Master for as long as possible. Why then, does he insist on bringing other women into their bed? And why can't he say he loves her?

As Dan battles his inner demons, Karen hopes a sexy mini break at the exclusive fetish club, Sugar Dust will allow them time to relax and reconnect. There she meets Beth, personification of Dan's past storming in to demolish her present. Can she show Dan that their relationship is strong enough to break the chains of his past, before Beth drives an immoveable wedge between them with her tales of what once was?

COMING SOON FROM RAVEN SHADOWHAWK

Slippers & Chains: Second Base

Dan and Karen kick off their new life together with a fabulous party in their new home. The night barely begins before old discomforts resurface, this time in the form of jealous best friends and unwelcomed family members. Karen, in the face of some life changing news from her mother, seeks comfort through the most effective means she knows; BDSM. But her desire to release her more dominant side clashes violently with Dan's inability to share what he feels to be his and his alone.

Can she prove to Dan that adding another facet to their D/s dynamic will do no harm to their relationship? And can she do it before his jealousy drives a wedge between them that nothing can pry free?

ABOUT RAVEN SHADOWHAWK

Raven ShadowHawk is one face of the author who writes fantasy under a second pseudonym. She is, according to most . . . okay, according to herself, the fun one of the pair.

Living in Leicester, UK with her partner (the Funk Master) and twin sons (Sprog 1 and Sprog 2), Raven writes erotica ranging from sensual and romantic to graphic and totally PWP.
Her interests include badly produced porn, chocolate, dressing up (particularly in matching underwear) and shouting at women who wear 'stupid shoes' and/or skinny jeans.

Discover more about Raven at www.ileandraXraven.co.uk or www.ravenshadowhawk.wordpress.com

Contact Raven via info@ravenshadowhawk.co.uk